Universal Threat

The Encounter Series

For Dean,

Enjoy!!

Hope you
love it!

Mary Anya

[signature]

2019

Universal Threat

The Encounter Series

Story by:

Margaret Traynor and Killarney Traynor

Written by :

Killarney Traynor

This is a work of fiction.

Names, characters, businesses, organizations, places, events, and incidents are either products of the author's imagination, or are used fictiously. Any resemblance to actual events, locales, organizations, or persons (living or dead) is entirely coincidental.

Cover designed by Killarney Traynor

Edited by Krista Burdine

Perhaps we need some outside, universal threat to make us recognize this common bond. I occasionally think how quickly our differences worldwide would vanish if we were facing an alien threat from outside this world.
    -   Ronald Reagan

CONTENTS

CAST OF CHARACTERS:

1985

Nicholas Miller, *college student, wanna-be US Marine*

Heather Miller, *high school student, Nick's sister*

Jeffrey Levinson, *high school student, Heather's friend*

PROLOGUE

Heather couldn't breathe. Terror rooted her to the ground and though her mouth hung open, she couldn't speak or scream. The alien hunter loomed closer, its shadow blocking the light of the dying sun, its body so close she could smell the tangy scent of fresh blood and feel the heat emanating from the enormous being. The alien's wheezing breath stroked her face and in the periphery of her vision, she could see the weapons hanging from its belt.

I'm going to die…

"Heather!"

She couldn't identify the voice or the hand that seized her wrist and yanked her out from under the looming threat. One minute she was rooted in place, the next she was running, trying frantically to keep up with the boys. Jeff was pulling her, Nick shoving them past him so that he could take up the rear, the pistol tight in his hand. The alien roared in tinny frustration and when Heather glanced behind, she saw the alien shrug the dead deer from its shoulders as it prepared to chase after them. Answering calls rang out from the clearing below.

"Go, go, *go!*" Nick shouted, shoving her.

They raced across the narrow top of the ridge and down the steep side. Fallen branches and low bushes reached to entangle their ankles. One took Jeff down and he landed spread eagle on the hard packed ground.

Heather stopped to help, but Nick shoved her again. *"Move it!"*

She stumbled forward, looking behind. The alien hunter had cleared the ridge and stood at the edge, getting its bearings. It held the deer limp in one hand. When it saw the boys, Nick tugging Jeff to his feet, it roared again. Then it lifted the animal by the two hind legs, whipped it over head, and threw it.

"Nick!" Heather screamed.

He saw it in time to duck and roll, Jeff duplicating the action in the opposite direction. The heavy carcass smashed into the ground between them with a sickening crunch, the limbs and head flopping loosely. Jeff's roll landed him at Heather's feet. She reached down to pull him up, keeping her eye on the ridge. The hunter turned to cry over its shoulder. Then it looked directly at Heather.

Jeff was saying, "…threw it like it weighed nothing…" but Heather wasn't paying attention. She was watching the hunter as it stepped backwards, preparing to spring.

"Jeff…"

The Hunter leapt, clearing yards, arms and fingers extended and for the first time, Heather saw the claws. The Hunter landed only inches away from the carcass, the ground shaking with its landing. On the ridge behind, the other alien appeared, armed and calling.

Nick gained his feet, pistol still in hand, blood from the carcass spattered across his face.

"Run!" he shouted and raised the gun.

Heather grabbed Jeff's arm and pulled him into the dense woods behind them. Shadows covered them and the sound of a pistol shot brought Heather to a halt. The alien's scream made her whip around. "Nick!"

There was a crashing sound and Nick appeared, wild-eyed. Behind him came the sound of splintering wood.

"Go go *go!*" he screamed.

Part One:
THE SIGHTING

CHAPTER 1

Columbus Day, 1985, a few hours earlier

It took over an hour to drive from the resort to the Stark Mountain trailhead and that meathead Jeff Levinson talked the whole way.

It wasn't that the driver, Nicholas Miller, objected to conversation. Nick himself was known to talk a blue streak about military history and tactics and had even challenged other boys on his college campus to debate about President Reagan's Strategic Defense Initiative (which, for the record, Nick was in favor of). Nick enjoyed talking and arguing with people who disagreed with him. He viewed the world and his life journey as a sort of obstacle course and relished every opportunity to sharpen his skills and hone his techniques. Normally, he'd encourage his passenger to talk.

That Columbus Day weekend, however, he was wondering exactly how much legal trouble he'd be in if he simply chucked Jeff out of a moving vehicle and left him for the park rangers to find.

Not that he could do that, of course, not with his kid sister, Heather, sitting in the middle and hanging on every word that gawky, goofy Levinson kid delivered like it was the gospel according to Jon Bon Jovi.

Jeff was a last-minute addition to the siblings' now-annual Columbus Day weekend hike. Heather had sprung the news on Nick only last night, a mere hour after Nick had arrived at the resort where the Millers and other assorted family members were enjoying their annual family reunion. When Nick complained that the last thing he'd wanted to do on his first break from college was escort Heather and her new boyfriend through the woods, his little sister turned red.

"He's not my *boyfriend*," Heather retorted hotly even as she blushed. "He's just a friend. He's new and he hasn't gone mountain climbing and I thought it'd be nice to show him around. Anyway, I thought you *liked* hiking."

There was nothing that Nick liked better, as well Heather knew, but that was entirely beside the point. "What do Mom and Dad think?" he asked.

She shrugged.

"He's just the new kid at school," she said, keeping her eyes on the floor. "And he needs a friend, that's all."

She looked so pathetic and sad that of course Nick gave in. But just because he had, it didn't mean he had to act like he liked the idea of this expedition.

"Fine, fine," he grumbled as he shoved the remainder of his clothes into the flimsy chest of drawers provided by the cabin company. "We hike. But *no* making out in front of me, got it? Or I'll have to string him up by his thumbs."

"I am *not* making out with Jeffrey Levinson!" Heather protested. She actually stomped her foot, her bouncy brown curls dancing with the effort. "We are just *friends*."

The funny thing was, Nick had believed her... until he met Jeff and his father, an older, carbon copy of the thin, geeky-looking kid. Jeff was tallish, with dark eyes hidden behind thick glasses, and he looked almost as nervous around Heather as she was around him. No one was fooled. Well, no one except perhaps Jeff's father, who was too busy making awkward small talk with Nick's parents to notice much of anything.

It was a relief to get out from under the parental gaze and into the truck, but they weren't halfway down the road when Nick discovered that he'd traded one set of awkward circumstances for another. Jeff Levinson was the type that covered his nerves by talking. So he talked.

He talked about his new camera, f-stops, lighting issues and the joys of dark room development. He talked about composition and the work done by artists that neither Nick nor Heather had ever heard of before. He talked about his comic book collection and his deep conviction that Planet of the Apes was misunderstood and ultimately deserved better treatment than the last few movies. He talked about *Star Trek: The Motion Picture* and why it was technically better than *Search for Spock*, though he admitted that the latter was more satisfying 'as a fan'. He talked and talked until Nick began to earnestly pray for a deer to jump out in front of the pickup and change the subject.

"I liked *Wrath of Khan* best," Heather said. She was toying with her long brown hair, her leg jiggling from nerves.

She'd been quiet for a long while, leading Nick to hope that her earlier enthusiasm had flagged. Now she shot Nick a nervous little look, as though pleading with him not to judge too harshly. He kept his eyes on the road.

"You liked *Wrath of Khan*?" This seemed to throw Jeff off his game for a minute. He pushed his over-sized glasses back up his nose and blinked at Heather. "Really?"

Nick was surprised, too. Until that moment, he hadn't known that Heather was more than superficially aware of the series. Nick himself had seen every movie and tried to catch the original show on re-runs, but though he, too, preferred *Wrath of Khan*, he wasn't about to jump into this conversation.

"Well, er, sure," Heather said, now sounding more uncertain. "It's, um, tense and full of deep themes. Like a submarine drama, only... you know, deeper." She was about to crash and burn. "It's about obsession and revenge and Nicholas Meyer is a genius... Um, isn't that what you think, Nick?"

Jeff looked at him now with curiosity and Nick shrugged. "It was all right," he admitted. He didn't know what else he could say without sounding like a nerd, so he kept quiet.

Heather shot him a disappointed look and Jeff, oblivious, went on to concede that, while *Khan* was a definite crowd pleaser, it did have its own drawbacks, especially when compared to other sci-fi films and TV shows, which he proceeded to outline in painstaking detail.

This was too much for Nick.

"So, Jeff," he said, cutting him off during a particularly onerous comparison of X-Wings to Colonial Vipers, "this is your first hike, isn't it?"

Jeff brightened.

"It's my very first!" he exclaimed and immediately launched into another monologue.

Jeff, having decided to go on this expedition into the wilds of northern New Hampshire (his phrasing), wanted to know everything he could about it. He wasn't afraid to ask questions; once he realized that Nick had spent his summer working for the parks department, the flow of queries came even faster. He asked about the roads and the parks. He wanted to know the different types of trees they drove past. He pondered at length about the changes in weather patterns and how they would affect the ecosystem. He asked about hunting, the method to gain permits, and how it served as a form of animal control.

"Has the state considered reintroducing wolves into the area?" he asked.

"Why should they?" Nick asked.

"Why, to rebalance the ecosystem, of course. I was reading a fascinating article about..."

Nick allowed his irritation to show. "I think the wildcats, the bears, and the hunters do a fair job of keeping the deer and moose populations in line."

"Wolves are magnificent creatures," Jeff mused.

"Not up close," Nick said, and Heather intervened to show Jeff the Old Man on the Mountain.

Nick sighed heavily. He didn't consider himself an over-protective brother by any means, but Heather *was* his only sister and there were limits. He'd taken one look at skinny, awkward, talkative, stuttering Jeff Levinson and thought, *She can do so much better.*

The Old Man on the Mountain served to distract Jeff only briefly. When he started in on the questions again, Heather again intervened and asked Jeff about his dad's work. Jeff talked about the protests at the nuclear sites and how, despite what detractors claimed, it was one of the safest forms of power known to man.

"That is," he admitted, "until we learn to harvest sunlight. That will be much cleaner and, ultimately the most effective source of power."

"Unless it rains," Nick commented and received a light punch in the arm from Heather.

"Scientists are developing ways to store sun-harvested energy in battery form, so that you won't suffer power loss when the sun goes down," Jeff said. "And when you think about the broader implications, there's a potential for individual households to never suffer from a power outage again. If each home provides its own power, they would be completely self-sufficient..."

"At least until the sun dies out," Nick interrupted.

Jeff blinked, taken off guard by the interruption. "What was that?"

"I *said*," Nick said, ignoring Heather's insistent elbow, "that we would be as long as the sun held out. Didn't one of the head eggheads in Washington say the sun was about to run out of fuel or something?"

"Well, that's pretty far into the future, and..."

"Creating a whole system of energy harvesting on something that is doomed from the start seems like a waste of time to me."

"Oh, but it isn't..."

"I mean, by the time everything got installed, *poof*, there goes the sun and you're done!"

"Well," Jeff said, trying to keep up with Nick's logic. "The sun isn't predicted to extinguish for at least…"

"Oh, lookee, there's our turn!" Nick called out, cheerfully cutting him off. "All right, boys and girls, it's time for us to go out into the wild!"

He took the turn sharply and immediately regretted the action, because doing so sent Heather sliding into the gangly egghead.

Awesome, he thought. *Just awesome.*

Mom and Dad hadn't been pleased at all when they learned about the planned hike. To their credit, they hadn't protested when first presented with the idea on Friday night. They'd been too busy with the reunion bonfire and meeting all their old friends and family, as both Nick and Heather had known they would be. But they had pulled Nick aside the next morning and gave him a list of 'dos' and 'don'ts'.

"You aren't to leave them alone for a second," Mom had said, her brown eyes dark with worry.

Dad had fixed Nick with The Look. "We aren't pleased at all with the timing of this thing, Nick. This is supposed to be family time, not necking time."

"Fred!" Mom had said.

"Dad, honestly!" Nick said. "Heather didn't tell me until last night and she'd already settled it with the guy. What was I supposed to do?"

"That's what we were asking," Mom said ruefully.

"Just keep them both out of harm's way." Dad clapped him on the shoulder. "We know we can count on you."

You sure can, Nick thought now. He and his father were of the same opinion when it came to Heather dating: she was entirely too young. And if convincing her meant that Nick had to lose a day hiking around a mountain to prove a young kid unworthy of her affections, he'd do it. And he'd picked the perfect trail to do it.

Heather'll hate me at first, he thought. *But she'll understand later. Hopefully.*

The path he was following was an unpaved access road, hardly visible from the highway, but well-known to the park rangers he'd worked with over the past year. It was tight and twisty. Branches raked the side of his father's over-sized truck and September's heavy rains had rutted the path so that it caused the cab to shudder like a popcorn popper. Heather braced herself against the dashboard, trying not to slide into one or the other of the boys. Jeff, gripping the overhead hand-hold, managed to say, "Are you *sure* this is a road?"

"Of course I'm sure!" Nick said. "I know every footpath and road on this side of the range."

"This – isn't – Lorne Mountain?" Heather managed through chattering teeth.

"No, it's Stark."

Her eyes went round as saucers. "Stark!"

"Stark," he confirmed and with another sharp movement of the wheel, slid the truck into a tiny gap in the trees. He braked and turned off the engine. "Ready to explore?" he asked.

Heather stared at him, open-mouthed.

"NICK!" she wailed.

"What's wrong?" Jeff asked.

"He's taken us to the wrong mountain!"

Jeff frowned. "Well, that's okay. It's not like I had my heart set on one or the other. Whichever you pick is fine, so long as I… Oh, look, a woodland creature!"

Before the two Millers would react, Jeff had snatched up his camera and bolted out the door. He hadn't reckoned on the proximity of the trees, however. His door smacked against a tree and rebounded on him, knocking him backwards into the truck. Hastily pulling himself together, he staggered forward, shutting the door on his coat by accident. When he'd finally extricated himself, he stumbled away from the truck, fumbling with his camera, tripping over fallen branches, and mumbling to himself about f-stops.

"What a dork," Nick said.

Heather whipped around, glaring at him furiously. "You... jerk!" she said.

He threw his hands up. "What did *I* do?"

"You told me we'd do Lorne Mountain, not Stark!" she said furiously.

"So I changed my mind. Big deal."

"Big deal?" she said. "You *know* Stark is a too hard a climb for a newbie. You're deliberately trying to make Jeff look foolish!"

Through the window over her shoulder, Nick saw Jeff, too focused on his new camera, get his foot tangled in a fallen branch and face-plant on the damp, leaf-covered ground.

"Honestly," he said. "I don't think he needs any help from me in that department."

Heather turned. Jeff was sitting up, waving to them.

"It's all right!" he shouted. "My camera's fine, but the northern goshawk I was trying to capture flew away. I don't suppose the nest is anywhere near here..."

His voice trailed off as he turned back toward the woods. Heather turned to Nick.

"The northern what?" she asked.

"He means a hawk," Nick said, a little nettled that Jeff had recognized and correctly named it. "Dork."

Heather opened her mouth to protest, but then shut it, defeated. Nick grinned and shoved his door open.

"Come on, kiddies," he shouted cheerfully. "We're burning daylight!"

It was, Nick decided, going to be a fun day after all.

CHAPTER 2

*T**his was a bad idea.*

The thought had been circling in Heather's head since the moment she'd first suggested the hike to Nick last night. Now it became a driving anthem, beating away into her subconscious. Nick had decided he wasn't going to like Jeff, even before he'd met him. But he'd shown his hand when he chose Stark Mountain instead of Lorne: he was trying to scare Jeff away from Heather.

He doesn't have to try that hard, Heather thought sourly, as she slipped out of the pickup truck. *Jeff hardly knows I'm alive. Not that I'm interested,* she amended her thoughts hastily. *Because I'm not. Not really.*

Even as she thought it, though, she knew better. Jeff Levinson had been on her mind ever since that first day in school, when he'd run into her and Margot in the hallway, knocking both of them down. It was an accident: he'd been studying his class schedule and hadn't seen them. That didn't stop Margot from tearing into him. Jeff had taken it meekly, almost dumbly, his dark gaze skipping from Margot's irate face to Heather's astonished one. He looked horrified and apologized profusely. He was so rattled that he even bowed before racing away from them to find the next class.

"What a dork," Margot had sniffed.

Heather couldn't agree. The image of the flustered young man with the glasses stuck in her head all day, complicating the already socially challenging adjustment of the first day of school. It was both a relief and a panic when she ran into Jeff again, this time in advanced mathematics. Without thinking, she'd taken the seat next to him and smiled when he looked at her, blinking.

"Heather Miller," she said, holding out her hand. When he showed no recognition, she elaborated, "We met. In the hall. You knocked us down like bowling pins."

He turned six shades of red.

"Oh!" he said. "Oh, good grief!"

He might have gone on gaping at her but fortunately Mr. Rice called the class to order. For the next forty-five minutes, Heather tried to focus on numbers and failed spectacularly, for it seemed whenever she stole a glance at Jeff, he was in the act of looking away from her. Then, once, quite by accident, they both looked at each other at the same moment. Heather smiled. Jeff looked astonished again, and then, slowly, he smiled back.

From then on, they were friends. Jeff was a scientist in the making, like his nuclear physicist father, and his desire to change the world made Heather's ambitions of becoming a veterinarian seem mundane and run of the mill. And yet they could talk for hours, and did whenever no one else was around. For reasons that Heather couldn't explain, Jeff was rapidly becoming one of the most important people in her life.

But they were NOT a couple. For all the time they spent together in school, whether in class or in home room or in the hallways, he never asked her out or even asked her to hang out. He seemed to forget about her the moment he walked away. This hiking trip, which was Heather's idea, was the first time they'd ever spent any time together outside of school grounds.

Margot thought it was a terrible idea.

"He's a nerd," she said. "He doesn't see anything but atoms and fusions and nuclear waste. Drop him. You should go out with Chris."

Chris Silva was the captain of the basketball team and a looker besides. Heather used to have a crush on him and still thought he was cute, but the idea of going out with him no longer excited her the way it used to. She didn't explain this to Margot, of course, partially because she was afraid that Margot was right: that Jeff only saw her as a friend and that she was making a fool of herself.

Now, as she stood by the truck, pulling her long hair into a pony-tail and watching Jeff stumble about the wood like an over-excited kid in a candy store, she wondered again if Margot and Nick were right.

If Jeff doesn't make a move by the end of today, I'm done, she thought. *I'll still be friends with him, but I'll move on.*

Ignoring the pang of her heart, she moved toward the back of the truck to help Nick.

***

Nick had brought the usual hiking kit, comprised of a few water bottles, a knife, a compass, a few food packets, and a first aid kit, most of which he carried in a well-worn denim backpack. He handed the water bottles to Heather and Jeff, who clipped them on to their jeans while Nick hoisted the backpack on-to his own back. It seemed heavier than normal, but Heather knew better than to inquire about the extra weight. The woods could be a dangerous place after all.

Stark Mountain was a fairly typical specimen of the White Mountains. Squat and craggy, with the tree-line ending about half-way up and giving way to bare granite, it gave the illusion of a gentle incline and an easy ascent. Barely half a mile along the path that Nick had chosen, the truth of the matter came out. Stark was, like all the New Hampshire mountains, riven with water-carved ditches, slippery with pine needles and fallen leaves, and subject to sudden, steep inclines. The path they were on was an old native trail, used for centuries and created by hearty souls accustomed to the rocky, root-infested terrain. It was not, as Heather well knew, a trail for amateurs, and yet Nick had chosen this one for Jeff's inaugural hike.

I should never have trusted him, she grumbled, as she followed Nick through the bends and curves of the narrow path. *I should have known he'd try to scare Jeff off.*

It was too late now. The day was too far gone to find another trail and arguing with Nick would only have made everything more awkward. Besides, Jeff hadn't complained. In fact, he'd been very excited when he learned that this trail had been in use since before the Revolution.

"Can you imagine that?" As his excitement grew, he sounded more and more like Jimmy Stewart. He came to an abrupt halt in the middle of the path and stood still, uncapping his lens. "How many feet have trod on this path? How many lives have been lived on this trail? This is a sort of living history we have here. Hang on a second – I want a picture."

"Picture of *what?*" Nick asked impatiently. "We haven't gotten to the scenic part yet."

"Of the trail," Jeff explained as he adjusted his lens. "It's for my grandmother. She's part Cherokee, you know."

"I didn't," Heather said. "That's cool."

"Nick, would you stand in the middle of the trail?" Jeff asked. "Maybe pose like you're hiking down it or something? Action shots are more interesting."

"Maybe you should pose in honor of your noble native ancestors," Nick suggested. "Of course, your moccasins would probably stand out."

He gestured to Jeff's neon colored and obviously bought-for-the-occasion sneakers. They were a little over-sized, Heather noticed, and Jeff seemed embarrassed when he glanced down at them.

"These are top of the line," he explained. "I was lucky to get them – they were the last the shop had yesterday."

"I'm not surprised," Nick said, ignoring Heather's scowl. "Come on, Geronimo, we're burning daylight and we haven't even started yet."

"Right," Jeff said. "Just one more shot."

He snapped it as Nick started off down the trail, whistling a tune from an old movie. Heather waited for Jeff, nervously clasping and unclasping her hands.

"We'd better hurry," she said, as he carefully put the cap back on his lens. "The trails out this way can be hard to follow and we don't want to lose Nick."

"Don't worry, Heather," Jeff said confidently. "I may not know much about mountaineering, but I was captain of the track team down south for two years in a row. If there's one thing I can do, it's move fast."

"You were on the track team?"

"Yes, ma'am," he said, with undisguised pride. They began to walk. The path here was level, with bends preventing them from seeing Nick up ahead. "Cross country and sprint."

"Wow. I didn't know you were so athletic."

"Well, I don't know that I'd claim that," he said modestly. "But I studied karate for a while, too."

"That's so cool! Like in the *Karate Kid*?"

"That's just movie karate," he said dismissively. "I study the real thing."

"Of course," Heather said, but she wasn't really paying attention. Relief flooded her system and her heart was singing. "Why haven't you signed up for the track team at school? They could sure use the help. Alvin was telling me that they haven't a prayer to win at any of their meets, now that Josh decided to switch to basketball."

She didn't say what she was also thinking: that it would make certain people in the school shut up if they saw Jeff wearing a school sports shirt.

"Well, now, I would, except that I made myself a promise," Jeff said. "I promised that this year, I was going to focus on academics and leave the sports to other people."

Her heart fell again.

"Really?" she said. "Why? I mean… I mean, you're already so smart. Don't you think you could… you know, do something else?"

"Not if I want to get into MIT." He turned to her, his eyes bright with enthusiasm. "Only the best and the brightest get in there and they turn out some of the world's best new engineers and scientists. It's where my parents went."

"Oh, really? That's awesome. Do you want to design ships or something?"

"Exactly! I want to work for NASA, helping design the new ships and find better ways to get to Mars. That's where the future is, you know. Space: the final frontier. It's where we'll have to go, after World War Three."

He said this so matter-of-factly that Heather shivered despite walking through the warm sunshine.

Of course, she thought sourly. *He would be thinking this, too.*

Though paranoia about nuclear warfare wasn't as high as it had been in the past, it was a nightmare frequently discussed and debated, especially since the erection of the nuclear plant in Seabrook. The president's announcement of the Strategic Defense Initiative – or *Star Wars* as the newscasters called it – had helped to revive some old fears.

"Where will you be when the apocalypse comes?" Margot had asked Heather only a few days ago. "That's the real question, isn't it?"

Margot was as certain that war was inevitable. Heather wasn't an idealist or a dreamer, but the general accepted certainty of imminent nuclear, apocalyptic war with the USSR was something that irritated and frightened her.

"Who says there's *has* to be another world war?" she snapped now.

Jeff looked at her, blinking.

"Well, everyone does," he said. "With all the nuclear arms stacked up and waiting, the world's a ticking time bomb."

"Well, I don't believe it." When he started to grin, she insisted. "I don't. We've had those bombs for forty years now and no one's used them since. Everyone *knows* that *everyone* will lose if we start a war, so no one is going to start one. War's not a foregone conclusion – it's only a possibility."

"No one knows when, of course, but with the current state of affairs…"

"The current state of affairs is Russia has bombs and we have bombs and neither wants to be annihilated. War's not fate. It's a choice."

"It's been made a few times," Jeff said. "The whole history of mankind is a history of war."

"And peace," Heather said. "But no one likes to focus on that. Peace is not as interesting as war."

She was trembling now. The anger had come on swift and ebbed as quickly, leaving her feeling embarrassed and exposed. Jeff had only been trying to explain why he wanted to get into MIT. He'd opened up to her and she'd shut him down. Now he was walking with his head down, his eyes on the ground, sober and serious as a judge.

She shouldn't have lost her temper and she wished she hadn't spoken at all. Now Jeff thought she was an idealistic fool who didn't have the courage to face facts.

I do! She thought fiercely. *But fear isn't fact. It's only emotion.*

Still, no good would come of arguing any further.

"I'm sorry, Jeff," she said after a moment. "It's just… Everyone keeps telling me we're all toast, and there's nothing we can do about it and that makes me mad. It's silly, I know. I'm sorry."

Jeff shook his head.

"You don't need to apologize," he said. "You're right. It is stupid to think it's inevitable. It doesn't have to be, I guess. Humans can make the right choices just as easily as they make the wrong ones. It isn't a given – just a possibility."

Relief washed over Heather. "Yes," she breathed. "That's what I think, too."

He grinned. "I guess I just like the idea of having an escape route. You know, like the escape pods in Star Wars. Just push a button and you can shoot out towards Tatooine."

Heather had seen the movie and had a vague recollection of what he was talking about, though the word 'Tatooine' meant nothing to her. But she was too relieved to admit ignorance, so she just grinned. "'You're my only hope,'" she quoted and was rewarded when his face brightened with recognition.

"You know," he said, putting a hand on her arm and pulling her to a halt. "That's not the only reason I want to work in the space program."

Suddenly he was standing really close, looming over her from his great height. He was so near that she could see that the worn leather cord around his neck, and the impression of a medallion pressing through the thin cloth of his shirt. His eyes were shifting nebulas of brown, green and tan. Heather could barely breathe.

"It... isn't?" she made herself ask. It was hard to speak.

Jeff nodded, his eyes shining. Then he leaned in even further and Heather felt as though her heart might pound through her chest cavity.

"No," he whispered. "I have this theory."

"Theory?" she asked automatically. She noted, with great interest, how his lips formed the words and how long his eye lashes were. "What theory?"

"About space," he said, even lower. "I haven't told this to anyone before, but I think..."

"HEY GUYS!"

Nick's roar cut through the moment like a buzz-saw at a tree-hugging party. Heather jumped back from Jeff, squeaking in alarm. Nick stepped out from the bend in the road and washed guilt over her.

Of all the bad timing...!

"What's the hold-up?" Nick demanded.

Jeff was awkwardly checking his camera, his movements jerky and nervous.

"N-nothing," he said. "Just talking."

Nick folded his arms and tried to pin Heather with a big-brother-knows-best look. "Talking?"

It was plain he didn't believe them.

I wish I could tell you differently, Heather thought. She glared as she answered, "Just talking, that's all. Jeff was telling me about MIT."

Nick looked over at Jeff suspiciously. "Oh really?"

Jeff looked up. He was calmer now, but his ears were tipped in pink. "Yes," he said. "I was telling her about my plans to work for NASA once I'm done with school." The very act of speaking revived his courage and he spoke faster, with more fervency. "You know, with the president's new initiative, the space program is as vital and important as ever before. I was reading this article in *Scientific American* that predicted that colonization is our best bet to handle the population explosion. There are unexplored opportunities opening up everywhere - and did you know most scientists predict we'll be on Mars by 2020?"

"You don't say?" Nick said, without a hint of interest. "I suppose you want to be one of the men on the expedition when that happens."

"Yes! How did you guess?"

"I figured it'd be the one thing you and I would agree on," Nick said. Then, before Jeff or Heather could figure out what he meant by that, he jerked a thumb over his shoulder. "Come on, space cadets, I have something you need to see."

"Right!" Jeff said.

"Coming!" Heather said.

Nick disappeared around the corner and Jeff hastened after him. Heather ground her teeth.

"Might as well have asked Dad to take us," she muttered, kicking at a pebble on the road. Then, realizing that both boys had left her alone in the middle of the road, she began to run.

At least it wasn't a total loss, she thought. *Wait till Margot hears about the track team and karate!*

That was a heartening thought.

When Heather rounded the bend, she found Nick crouched down at the side of the road, pointing to something. Jeff stood over him, absorbed in observation.

Heather ran up and tapped Nick on the shoulder.

"Did you know that Jeff runs track?" she asked, breathless. "He was *captain* of his team!" When Nick looked up at her, his blue eyes crinkled with concern, she added, "*And* he's studying karate!"

Nick's eyes shifted from her to Jeff. "Karate, huh? That's hand-to-hand, right?"

"Sometimes weapons are used, too," Jeff said, with a show of modesty. "I'm on track to start learning how to use nun-chucks pretty soon."

"Cool," Heather breathed and Jeff blushed.

Nick got up, brushing the dirt from his knees. "I don't suppose you brought any of these nun-chucks with you, did you, Levinson?"

Jeff looked confused. "Well, no," he said. "They aren't exactly... I mean, they're not really for the forest. It's, uh, basically two sticks chained together and you sort of whip them over your head. Good in the city, but around trees..." Jeff's voice trailed off. He gestured to the branches overhead and shrugged. "No good, you know?"

Nick rubbed his head. "Well, that is too bad. Take a look."

He gestured to the ground where a pile of scat lay, half covered by fern leaves. Heather bent over to take a look and her heart, so light a moment ago, sank into her feet. She knew what it was immediately.

"Good grief," Jeff said, making a face. "Some people have no decency..."

Nick cut him off. "That's not human, Levinson."

Jeff looked at him wide-eyed. "Not... human?"

"It's a bear, Jeff," Heather said, annoyed with Nick.

"Bear?!?" Jeff turned pale as a sheet. "There are *bears* around here?"

"Just black bear. They're pretty small."

"Small? Like, how small? Like Teddy Bear small? Ewok small?"

"Ewok!" Nick scoffed. "Jeez, man!"

"How small?" Jeff demanded.

"Couple hundred pounds," Heather admitted. "But this is a few days old, Jeff, and they're probably just looking for shelter. It's getting close to hibernation time."

"So all they are looking for," Jeff said bitterly, "is a bedtime snack."

Nick exchanged looks with Heather. "If it makes you nervous, Levinson, we can turn back and go home."

"Of course it doesn't make him nervous!" Heather interjected. She got up and stood between the pair of them. "Jeff isn't afraid of a little bear, are you, Jeff? Besides, they have lots of bears down south. Don't they, Jeff?"

"Sure." Jeff's affirmation wasn't quite as enthused as Heather's. "Lots of them, especially in the Carolinas and, er, Virginia."

Nick folded his arms. "So we go on, then?" he said.

"Sure," Heather said.

"I haven't gotten my mountain view yet," Jeff said.

Nick shrugged. "Okay, then," he said. "But just keep in mind that this isn't our territory, it's theirs. So we stay alert and close together, right?"

"Right," Heather echoed.

"Absolutely," Jeff said. When Nick's back was turned, he whispered to Heather, "Who is this 'they' he's talking about?"

"The animals, of course," she whispered back. "But don't worry. If you don't bother them, they won't bother you. Usually."

"Usually," Jeff repeated. "Got it."

He looked worried and suddenly Heather found herself wondering if he was even capable of hiking the mountain. Jeff was a city kid after all, and the discovery of scat seemed to really frighten him. Maybe Nick's unspoken criticisms about Jeff were right and she'd been...

Then Jeff turned to her, his face wreathed in grins.

"Say, Heather!" he said.

"Say what?" she responded.

"If we do happen to see a bear, imagine what a shot that would be!" and he raised the camera on his neck and gestured with it. "First place for sure, if we survived the encounter!"

Heather grinned back, relieved. "Definitely."

CHAPTER 3

The trail wound through trees and boulders, looping ever higher, growing steeper as they moved along. Overhead, tall pines and squat maples rustled in the chill, October breeze. Most of the leaves had already fallen, but they could still catch glimpses of orange among the dull pine green. Flocks of south-bound birds filled the skies overhead while below, the woods were noisy with sounds of tiny skittering footsteps on crisp leaves and falling acorns and pinecones.

It's a perfect day, Heather thought, as she scrambled to catch up to Nick's long striding pace. *Absolutely perfect.*

As she thought this, she removed the scarf from around her neck and tucked it into one of the large pockets in her jacket. It was warm for October and the exercise was making it feel even more so. Nick, loping on ahead, had already removed his hat and would probably end up tucking his jacket into the backpack.

I hope he was right about the bear scat being a few days old, she thought. But of course, he must be. He'd spent the entire summer working with the rangers, all of whom sent glowing reports home about his hard work and quick learning ability. It surprised no one who knew him. Nick had been born for the outdoors, with his sharp eyes, quick instincts, and strong, lithe frame. He wasn't tall, but he was strong and he enjoyed every kind of outdoor activity, from building a tree-house with their father to going on long lonely rambles in the woods. He'd learned to hunt with their uncles and knew everything there was to know about wild turkeys and deer and fish and how to prepare them.

Nick had always been a woodsman, just as he had always wanted to go into the army, although their parents objected to the latter. Going to college was a deal that he'd made with their father, agreeing to try it out for two years before signing up. Their parents were hoping that Nick would eventually change his mind. Heather knew Nick better than that. He would stick out the college years out of respect for their parents, but the minute his obligation was done, he'd be signed up, no matter how Heather wished it were different.

Bother it! Heather thought.

She'd never wanted to go into the military and though she loved the outdoors fully as much as Nick did, she'd never wanted to become a ranger either. Heather had loved working with animals, whether it was dog-sitting for her neighbors or volunteering with the horses at Chase Farm. If she could pass the necessary tests, she would be going to veterinary school when she was done high school. It wasn't as cool as the military, maybe, or as glamorous as the job Jeff would probably end up with, but it was a career that excited her and that was all that mattered.

Probably all that mattered. Her mother worried about the cost of the long years of training and Aunt Doris predicted that Heather would switch majors before the end of the first school year.

"Cut open one jack rabbit and then see how bad you want it!" she'd said, well knowing how sick Heather had been during frog-dissection day at school.

Maybe Aunt Doris was right. Maybe she wasn't. But college was still some distance away and Heather made it a policy never to worry about something until it was right in front of her. She wasn't always good at keeping that policy, but today she would be.

The climb was getting steep. Gaps in the tree line on their left revealed that they had climbed to a good height, though Heather knew they were still a long way from the best views. She glanced behind her to see how Jeff was doing, and then called ahead to Nick. "Hold up! We lost him again!"

Nick's muttering floated back down on the breeze to her. "Friggin' tourists!"

They found Jeff a few yards back, laying on his stomach, squinting through the viewfinder into the bushes.

"What *are* you doing?" Nick asked.

Jeff waved for silence. The siblings looked at each other, then dropped to their stomachs and crawled over on either side of him. He waved again impatiently and they stopped and focused along the line of his lens. He had pointed it into the bushes, a mixture of ferns and scrubby wild blueberries. There was nothing of particular interest that Heather could see, and when she looked over Jeff's head at Nick, his shrug told her he was flummoxed too.

"What is i-?" she started to ask, only to receive a panicky wave for silence.

Nick rolled his eyes and dropped his head on his hands.

The quiet stretched. Heather lay on her stomach, listening to it rumble and wishing that Jeff would just take his picture so they could move on.

"Dude," Nick said, but Jeff said, "Shh!" and a moment later snapped the photo.

"Got it!" he crowed and the sound, after so much quiet, was like the crack of a gun. He rolled on to his back and up to his feet, grinning like a prize winner.

"Got *what?*" Nick hopped up too. "A leaf?"

"Well, I got that too," Jeff admitted, taking out the cloth to carefully wipe his lens for what must have been the fifth time that day. "But my focus was the inchworm on the leaf."

He beamed at them. Nick stared back.

"The *inchworm?*" he asked.

"Yes. I thought it might make an interesting subject."

"For what?"

Now it was Jeff's turn to look confused. "For a picture," he said.

"Jeff's trying to tap into his creative side," Heather explained.

"Your creative side," Nick repeated. "I thought you wanted to be a scientist."

"I do," Jeff said. "But I can't decide if I want to get into quantum physics or if possibly astrophysics would better suit my particular suite of skills..."

"What do creative pictures have to do with quantum physics?" Nick interrupted. "Isn't science all, like, math?"

"Science isn't math. It's the mechanics of the universe. It is problem solving and star gazing, creating cures for cancer and figuring out the trajectory of the sun. It is studying brain waves and harnessing ocean waves for fuel. It's the study of everything, from human nature to extraterrestrials. It's learning about..."

"Hang on right there." Nick put his hand out to stop the flow of words. "Extraterrestrials?"

"Yes." Jeff blinked. "You know... aliens."

"I know what they *are!*" Nick snorted. "I mean, I know what they are on TV, but no one really *believes* in them, right?"

"I don't know what faith has to do with it," Jeff said cagily.

"I'm not talking about faith," Nick said. "I'm talking about UFOs and little green men and Roswell and Area 51. It's all nonsense. No one has *ever* been able to prove they exist."

"No one's ever proven that they don't," Jeff said. "I'd say there's a very good chance that they do exist."

Now they both gawked at him.

"Come *on!*" Nick said. "That's loony!"

"Jeff, really." Heather rubbed her arms against a sudden chill. It was bad enough to believe that the Russians in the

USSR were ready to level the planet with nukes. Believing in otherworldly forces, even for a second, was too much.

But Jeff didn't seem at all put out by their disbelief. He began to stride up the trail, wiping his lens as he spoke. The other two fell into step with him.

"I don't see why it's such a crazy idea," Jeff said. "It's simple math. Think about it: we already know that the universe is made up of thousands of solar systems, and that there are potentially millions of planets in those systems, all of them going around a sun or star. Of those millions of planets, its logical to assume that some, like Earth, are orbiting around a sun at suitable distance to allow for growth. Given the right ingredients, life will form. We know this is possible, because we ourselves are the proof. Given the amount of planets and suns that are out there, I think assuming that Earth is the only one sustaining life is ridiculous at best and egotistical at worst."

"Egotistical?"

"Sure. For hundreds of years, humans thought that the sun revolved around Earth. Science proved them wrong. We weren't the center of the system – the sun is."

"What does that have to do with aliens existing?" Nick scoffed. "Conventional wisdom states that we are the only beings around. Only kooks think otherwise."

"It's an example," Jeff said. "Conventional wisdom said Earth was the center once. It was wrong. It's likely to be wrong in this case too."

"But if they did exist," Heather said, "wouldn't we know about them by now? Wouldn't they have reached out to us in some way?"

"That's presupposing that they are more advanced than we are," Jeff said. "We've only just gotten to the moon. Another planet may be younger, with only amoeba living at present. Lack of contact isn't proof."

"So, let me get this straight," Nick said. "You think aliens exist."

"To be more precise," Jeff said, "I think it highly unlikely that we are the only beings in the universe."

"So… you think it was a UFO in Roswell?"

"That," Jeff said severely, "was a military test gone wrong. Only the fringe element thinks there was anything behind that."

"Only the fringe element thinks that aliens exist at all," came the rejoinder. "What makes your conventional wisdom right and mine wrong?"

"The math is on my side," Jeff said.

"But *you* just said math isn't science."

"It isn't. Any more than a hammer is a house. It's a tool with which to build a house, but it is as much apart from it as the builder is. Essential, but apart." Suddenly, Jeff's eyes brightened. "Oh, is that the view?"

With a burst of childish energy, he darted ahead of them to where a bend in the trail opened up into a valley view of the mountain range. Nick and Heather let him go, watching him as he peered out over the edge.

"Oh my gosh!" Jeff called back to them. "This is *magnificent!* You both should come and see!"

He began snapping pictures rapidly.

"If he thinks that's good, wait 'til he gets to the top," Heather said, shoving her hands in her pockets.

Nick looked at her narrowly. "He's crazy, sis. You know that, right? Absolutely round the bend."

"He is *not,*" she insisted. "He's just… you know. Watched too many episodes of *Logan's Run* or something."

"Hey, guys!" Jeff crowed. "If you lean out far enough, you can hear your voice echo!"

"Loony," Nick said. "He probably believes he's that guy from *The Invaders.* Vincent, or something. The only one on the planet who believed in aliens. No one else believed David Vincent and all the proof disappeared whenever the aliens were defeated. As far as we know, David Vincent was just a crazy person and the show was all about his delusions."

Heather hesitated. In normal, sane, and sensible situations, no one admitted to believing in alien life. But not only had Jeff done just that, he'd actually gone so far as to defend the position. Either he was on to something or Nick was understating the case.

I should be glad this came out now, before I got too involved, she thought and knew immediately that this information made no difference at all.

So she looked at Nick and lifted her chin.

"He's not crazy, Nick," she said, in as loud a whisper as she dared. "He's just a little… eccentric. And there's nothing wrong with that."

"Nothing *wrong* with being a loony tune?"

"No. We're all weird in our own way. Einstein never brushed his hair, right?"

Now he was staring at her as though she were crazy.

"Good grief, Heather," he said. "You're really round the bend."

"Maybe," she said. "But Jeff is *my* guest and you promised you'd be nice."

"I promised no such thing. I said I'd take you guys hiking. I didn't say I'd play Captain Kirk to his Spock. If he keeps talking crazy-like, I'm going to leave him here for the bear."

"Nick!"

"We'd better keep going," Jeff called back. "It's getting late. Come along, you two, let's shake a leg."

And he disappeared up the trail.

Nick ground his teeth. "Of course," he said. "I may end up leaving him here anyway."

CHAPTER 4

They kept climbing and no one spoke about aliens again. The further they traveled, the steeper the trail grew and the more excited Jeff became. He darted back and forth between the pair of them, asking Nick about the sights, Heather about the plants, and keeping up a running commentary on his discoveries along the way.

"I can see why you enjoy the mountains, Nick," he even said at one point. "It's so peaceful around here."

"I once thought so, too," Nick said. "Mind the doo – Too late."

They found more evidence of animals as they went along. Heather found deer tracks and Jeff claimed he'd discovered more bear dung, only to be corrected by Nick.

"Not bear," Nick grunted. "Coyote."

"Coyote! I thought they were out west."

"They are. They're also here."

Jeff bent over his discovery, his nose wrinkled in disgust. "How can you tell them apart?"

"Three months intensive training with the park rangers," Nick said. "Also, those prints over there." He pointed out the clawed markings a short distance away.

A little further along the trail, Nick came across evidence of a scuffle – torn up dirt and leaves, a bush with broken branches.

He stayed to examine this further while Jeff and Heather continued up the path. When Nick caught up with them a short time later, he looked pensive. Jeff was taking a picture by the edge of the path and telling an apparently hilarious story about his last science experiment in Florida. Heather was standing off to the side, biting her lip. Nick pulled her further away and spoke low.

"Looks like there was a fight and the deer got away," he said.

"Bear or coyote?"

"Coyote," he said. "I can't tell how many, but the deer was still relatively small."

"How fresh?"

"Yesterday, I think."

"Oh. Oh, geez."

"Yeah. Look, Heather, it'll be fine, really. They won't bother us and even if they do…" He swung the backpack off his pack and unzipped the front pocket. She recognized the glint of dark metal, even though he only gave her a glimpse before he closed the pocket again.

"Dad's gun," she said.

He shook his head and swung the backpack back on. "Mine. I told Dad I was bringing it along." She must have looked even more concerned, because he reached out to pat her shoulder. "Take it easy, kid. I'm just letting you know to make you feel better."

"You don't think we're in danger then?" she asked.

He shrugged. "Coyote usually keep to themselves." He glanced over his shoulder at Jeff. "Just keep the pistol a secret from the Martian hunter, okay? I've got the feeling he'd be more nervous knowing I have it than you would be thinking I didn't."

The camera dangled around Jeff's neck as the gangly tourist bent over his notebook. His forehead puckered in concentration as he made a meticulous mark on the page.

Heather turned to Nick. "Have you noticed anything about him, Nick?"

"Sure, a lot of things. He's tall, awkward, nerdy, and annoying, for a start."

"I mean," she said, keeping her temper firmly in line. "He talks about his dad all the time. It seems like they spend all kinds of time together when he isn't working. But the only thing Jeff's ever told me about his mother is that she went to MIT. Don't you think that's strange?"

Nick shrugged. "Heather, everything about that dude is strange."

Something about that was moderately comforting. She folded her arms and nodded. "You know, he doesn't want to work for NASA just to find aliens."

Nick gave her a 'why would I care about this' look, but she pressed on, determined. "He thinks the only way humanity can survive a nuclear holocaust is if we, like, have somewhere else to go."

To her surprise, Nick actually seemed impressed. "That's one way to handle the situation," he mused, casting a more appraising look towards Jeff. "Though we are *years* away from being able to get anywhere beyond the moon, let alone colonize. Right now the best way to ensure survival is to be prepared to strike first."

Heather's fists tightened. "Then you think war is inevitable, too. War and annihilation."

"War is, definitely. Why do you think I want to sign up? You don't just stock nuclear arms for fun, you know." He shoved his hands into his pockets and sighed. "Look, I know you don't like thinking about this, Heather, and honestly, I don't like it any more than you. But someone has to be practical and prepared. We can't all live with our head in the clouds. Idealists are far more dangerous than realists." He glanced up at the sky. "We'd better keep moving if we want to make the summit and back before dark."

"Sure," Heather said. She felt numb, but the last thing she wanted was to be out on the trail at night.

Nick strode off, calling to Jeff to come along. He did, willingly, and began to talk about something to do with dark rooms and solutions.

Heather wasn't listening. She was thinking about war and Reagan and the Iron Curtain and the Arms Race and the inevitability of war. The USSR and the USA were two opposing ideologies whose only way to grow was in the absence of the other. Everyone thought so, even if they didn't talk about it. Nick and Jeff, the warrior and the scientist, both examined the situation from their respective view points and came to the same conclusions as the political analysts. But even though she had to admit the facts favored that conclusion, Heather couldn't make herself believe in the same thing.

It doesn't have to happen, she thought. *Surely there's another way. War doesn't have to be the answer. We still have a choice. So long as we can think and feel and talk, we have a choice.*

Mom thought the same as she, but like Heather, she didn't talk about it much to others.

"You grow tired of talking to walls," she'd explained to Heather once. "But just because I can't say what I think doesn't mean I agree with anything else anyone is saying. And I'll bet lots of other people feel the same way, too."

There was some hope in that.

"...just like in that episode of *The Twilight Zone,* when those three guys got a hold of a camera that took pictures from the future," Jeff was saying enthusiastically.

Heather shook her head and looked at him. "The future?"

"Sure. Don't you want to know what the future holds, Heather?"

She shook her head firmly.

"No," she said. "If it's anything like you and Nick expect, I'd rather remain in complete ignorance."

And she marched on, leaving a bewildered Jeff behind her.

CHAPTER 5

It took them another forty minutes of hard work to reach the next vantage point. The trees were thinning out and the path was rocky and steep. A few places they had to use their hands to keep going. Heather's shirt became sticky with sweat and her calf muscles ached, but it was a good ache, the ache of achievement. She began to relish the climb itself and found herself looking forward to the view from the top, which she hadn't seen in ages.

Jeff grew quieter as the hard work of the climb absorbed his concentration. Nick took to the mountain like a machine. There were no more signs of wild carnivores, not that there would be. Heather knew that coyotes and bears stayed in the forested areas where their prey lived and hid, and the further they climbed, the further she put the animals from her mind. Higher was safer and she could forget their presence on the way back.

Nick, in the lead, called back: "Let's stop at the next scenic point for a minute."

"Sure," Heather said.

Jeff just waved a hand in assent.

The scenic point was a slight detour, a granite outcropping that overlooked the valley, the river, and the mountains beyond. It was a good spot for a picture, Heather knew, and a good place to sit and rest. But she'd forgotten just how vast the view actually was. Jeff's mouth dropped when he caught sight of it.

"Holy guacamole!" he said. "Holy Toledo."

"Dude, really?" Nick exclaimed. "Don't you even know how to swear like a normal person?"

Jeff didn't respond. He ran to the edge and looked over. Heather went up beside him and her stomach dropped when she saw the height and the sheer edge below. A valley stretched out below them with a river winding through a sea of green pines, orange and red maples, and yellow birches. Over the trees, a flock of geese flew in perfect formation. Beyond them, the White Mountains rose like steel and green walls, rugged and squat and wild.

"It's really beautiful," Jeff said. He sounded surprised. "I had no idea."

Heather's heart swelled with pride.

"We like it," she said. When he looked at her, she pointed to a spot on the mountain side. "One of my uncles has a hunting cabin around there."

"A hunting cabin!" He made it sound like a Swiss chalet, exotic and desirable. "What a grand idea."

"There are lots of those around here," Nick said. He stood with his arms folded, surveying the valley he'd come to know intimately over the past few years. "Some legal, some illegal."

"Really?"

"They're easy to put up," Heather said. "That is, if you don't care about modern comforts. A lot of them are just shacks made out of pine logs. They're neat, but not too comfortable."

"Unless you're caught in a sudden snow storm," Nick said with a grin. "Then they'd rival the Ritz."

"You get those around here?" Jeff asked. "Sudden storms?"

"In the winter, obviously," Nick said.

"Obviously," Jeff said without rancor. He looked out over the valley again with a happy expression on his face. "What a hearty race you all must be."

There seemed no good response to that. Nick turned to go, saying, "We're still a ways from the top…"

"Just a second!" Jeff held out the camera. "Photo op. Heather, stand here and I'll get a picture of you, too."

Heather, painfully aware of her bedraggled appearance, posed at the edge of the ledge. Watching Jeff snap a picture, Nick's words kept cycling through her head: *"He probably believes he's that guy from The Invaders. Vincent, or something, the only one on the planet who believed in aliens. As far as we know, David Vincent was just a crazy person and the TV show was all about his delusions."*

How can you tell if a person's crazy or not? How can you tell anything about a person?

Jeff raised his head and grinned at her.

"What a view," he said and for a moment, her heart lifted.

Don't be silly, she thought. *He's talking about the valley.*

She offered to take a picture of him against the valley. "For your grandmother," she said. Delighted with the idea, he surrendered the camera and darted over to the edge.

"Hold it," she said and snapped a picture. "Fine – now do a pose."

"A pose?"

"Hurry up, Heather!" Nick called.

"Just a second," she said and grinned at Jeff. "Yeah, pose like an explorer. Like Indiana Jones… you know!"

He thought about it a second, then turned, propped one foot on a rock, and leaned forward, looking out over the valley. "Like this?"

"Perfect!" She snapped the photo, giggling. From behind her, she heard Nick's exaggerated sigh. From the expanse in front of them, the sound of honking geese died away, to be replaced by the whine of a distant airplane. "Do another!"

"Okay…"

Jeff looked around for inspiration. The airplane sound was growing exponentially louder. Nick stepped to Heather's side, scanning the skies. She looked, too, but could see nothing.

"Awfully close…" Nick muttered.

"But where is it?" she responded.

"How's this, Heather?"

Jeff had turned and was peering over the edge in an exaggerated fashion, one hand shading his eyes. The whine of the engine, high pitched and piercing, covered everything. Nick said something, but his voice was lost.

Then the ship screamed right past them, so close they could feel the warmth of the huge machine. It sucked at the air, whipping the trees and dust up in a whirl-wind. The pull was so strong that Heather stumbled forward, losing her grip on the camera and stumbling to her knees. Jeff shouted. Nick was on the ground, shielding his eyes against the churned-up dirt and shouting at something ahead of him. She looked. The ledge was empty – Jeff was gone.

As suddenly as it came, the windstorm stopped and the ear-piercing sound receded. Nick jumped to his feet and ran to the edge, shouting, "Jeff? *Jeff!*"

Heather was right on his heels, her heart in her throat, choking off her ability to speak. *No, no, no! Jeff!*

A hand appeared, clutching at the ground before it disappeared again. They raced to the edge. Heather fell to her knees and looked over the side. Jeff was standing shakily on a slippery outcropping of dirt, just under the ledge's edge. How he'd managed to land and stay there, without the outcropping giving way under the sudden impact, Heather couldn't fathom, but she was too busy being grateful to ask questions.

Thank you, thank you, thank you, God!

"You all right there, buddy?" Nick asked.

"What was that?" Jeff shook his head, as though to shake something out of his ears. "What happened?"

"Don't step back!" Heather shrieked.

Jeff froze, his face white with the realization of how close he'd come to falling. He looked up at Nick and his voice rose to a near-squeak. "Can't you get me up there?"

Nick reached down and Jeff grabbed his hand in a white-knuckled grip, using his other hand to clutch an exposed root like his life depended upon it. As there was nothing between him and a drop of a thousand feet, Heather couldn't blame him.

"Give me your other hand," Heather instructed.

Jeff looked at her and tugged on the root.

"I can't let go," he confessed.

"Heather," Nick said. "Get behind me. Grab hold of that tree," he indicated a sturdy white birch, "and grab my belt with your other hand."

She knew at once what he was trying to do. He wanted to make sure that when he hauled Jeff up, he didn't lose his footing on the slippery forest bedding of pine needles and leaves. And he didn't want to say so plainly, for fear of freaking Jeff out.

We could lose him, she thought. *Nick could fall, too.*

She shook the thought off quickly – there was no time to panic. She ran to the birch and, thinking quickly, tugged her own belt off and wrapped it around the tree to get a better grip. Nick nodded and dropped to his knees. She did the same and caught hold of his belt.

Jeff was talking, his voice a nervous stream of conscious.

"…just rushed over me and I lost my footing and all I could think of was, Jeff, old man, you've had it, you're done for, and you haven't even finished your dissertation on quantum…"

"Levinson," Nick said, but the rambling went on.

"…I'd promised to return it by the fourth, but life got in the way, as they say, and…"

"Levinson…"

"…and what does he expect me to do, drop everything for chance to play third stringer on a second rate…"

"JEFF!" Nick roared. "For God's sake, man, *concentrate!*"

There was a moment, then Heather heard Jeff say contritely, "Concentrate. Got it."

Nick sighed and glanced back at Heather. His face was strained.

"Okay, Levinson," he said, his voice low and steady. "We're going to start pulling you up, but you have to climb to help us, okay?"

Heather could only see the top of his curly head as Jeff looked wildly back and forth.

"Climb," he said, as though dry-mouthed. "Up. Right."

"Don't look down," Heather called.

Jeff laughed nervously. "Too late. You know, if you look carefully, you can actually see where the glacial movements of the…"

"Dude," Nick said sternly. "Forget the geology and start climbing."

He did. It was slippery work, for the granite face was smooth with little to grab on to. Nick's arms were taut with the strain. When Jeff slipped and nearly fell, they all shouted and Heather's heart squeezed so tight she felt it would explode. But he made it. Nick, with Heather's help, pulled him half way, allowing Jeff to throw a long leg up on to flat surface. In a second, he was up and they all collapsed in relief on the ground.

"That," Jeff observed, "was the most frightening thing that ever happened to-" He was cut off when Heather threw her arms around him in a tight, frightened hug.

"You could have *died*," she exclaimed. Tears threatened to fall, but she held them in tight.

"You're telling me," Jeff said. His arms gently held her for a fraction of a moment before he pulled back again, his eyes on her face.

"It was a close call," he said softly.

Heather was about to lose herself in his dark eyes when Nick's snort cut through the moment.

"Closer than you know, Levinson," he said. "Who'd have thought such a skinny dude could weigh so much? And what was all that stupid talk about glacial movements?"

Heather tore her gaze from Jeff and wrapped her arms around herself. *Be cool, Heather!*

"I was just thinking of the ice age," Jeff responded.

Nick looked at him. "You were hanging from the side of a cliff, thinking about the *ice age?*"

"It seemed a better idea than thinking about hanging from a cliff's edge." Jeff leaned over Nick to point. "Actually, speaking of mass movement, as I was saying earlier, if you look really closely…"

Once again, Heather cut him off. "Look!" she shouted and jumped to her feet, pointing in the opposite direction. "The plane!"

From a distance away, a thin column of smoke was rising, billowing and shifting in the autumn breeze. A line had been sliced through the once unbroken sea of orange and yellow leaves, leading from the smoke plume almost directly to where they were standing. The plane must have dropped fast, for it had cut a short path skimming the side of the mountain, coming to rest in a relatively high flat. Nothing else indicated tragedy. The breeze rustled the leaves, the departing geese honked, and the forest seemed as it had been.

Nick rolled over and hopped up to his feet to stand beside Heather. He scanned the scene, his eyes narrowing as he made calculations. Jeff shakily stood, too, taking a step or two even further back from the ledge.

"How far are they?" Heather asked.

"From here, I can get there in twenty minutes," Nick said. He looked at the pair of them. "Little longer with you two along."

"That quickly?"

"I know this area," Nick said and pointed. "There's another path that cuts right across."

"You've got the first aid kit?"

"Of course."

Heather nodded. "Okay, let's go then."

"Wait!" Jeff called, stepping forward as Nick swung the backpack up on his back. "Shouldn't we go get some help?"

"They probably already radioed a mayday," Nick said. "Besides, it'll take us two hours to get to the truck, another hour to get to the nearest station, after which it'll take the Rangers at least a few hours to get here."

"By then it might be too late," Heather explained.

"But… But…" Jeff said. He looked uneasily over his shoulder. Heather felt a sudden pang of mixed emotions – sympathy, for Jeff was just recovering from a shock, and annoyance, because he was holding up a rescue mission.

"I know what to do," Nick said calmly. "Heather does too: she's gotten some first aid training. We'll get to the wreck and once there, if they don't have a working radio, I'll head back for the rangers. But let's get there first, right?"

Jeff looked from one to the other, and then nodded.

"Okay," he said. "Let's go."

"Right," Nick said. "Heather, stick close to me. Levinson, bring up the rear and keep an eye out."

Jeff seemed resigned. "Right!" he said and saluted.

Heather handed him the camera and then they both followed Nick off the beaten trail and into the woods.

CHAPTER 6

Nick didn't run, exactly, but he kept a swift pace through the woods. If there was a trail, Heather couldn't see it. She stayed between the two boys, watching her step through the tangled underbrush and bringing to mind everything she'd ever learned about first aid from her years as a Girl Scout, then a Life Guard at the pools in Exeter. Her training, thorough enough for the occasional camping trip and kiddie pool trauma, seemed woefully below grade now.

"Nick!" she called, ducking under a branch. "What size was the plane?"

Nick, several yards ahead, said, "What?" in a distracted tone.

"The plane – what size?"

"I dunno. What difference does it make?"

"I didn't see it," she said and looked over her shoulder. "Jeff?"

He shook his head. "Nope. Too busy falling."

"*None* of us saw it?"

"Looks that way," Nick said.

That was strange. She scoured her memory, trying to think of that moment when the plane passed. It had been so close. Surely she must have seen something to help identify it – a flash of a tail, perhaps, or the tip of a wing. But she could remember nothing at all.

Nick came to an abrupt halt, studying his compass. Heather and Jeff, both breathless, stopped next to him. Heather shook her head, lifting her hair from her neck so that the breeze could cool it.

"That's so weird," she said aloud. "One of us should have seen something."

"Yes," Jeff said, musing. "I was thinking the exact same thing."

"It doesn't matter," Nick snapped, looking up and around. "It doesn't matter what it looks like, so long as we can get to it."

Heather looked around. They had gone downhill from the ledge, a steep and tricky descent that left her feeling lucky no one had tripped or twisted an ankle. Now, though still high up, they were on a level bit of ground, traveling more slowly because of the dense underbrush. The trees were young and thick here. They'd lost sight of the crash site the moment they left the ledge, relying on the smoke plume to guide them. Now, under the pines and maples still crowded with red leaves, the plume was harder to make out, leaving them to rely on Nick's innate sense of direction. A sense which seemed to be eluding him now.

"Are we lost?" Jeff asked, tactlessly.

Nick glared at him. "I know where we are," he said. "It's just getting to the crash site..." He looked around and pointed to the right, where the mountain rose like a wall. "We go that way."

He started without waiting for their agreement. Heather and Jeff exchanged looks and hurried after him.

The climb was steep, steeper than the trail, requiring hands and knees. Nick kept the pace brisk and Jeff stayed close behind Heather, offering her a hand up from time to time. They reached a ridge in short order and followed it until they reached a gap in the tree line.

"There!" Jeff pointed.

The smoke plume was fainter now. The wind had dispersed it and it seemed the fire, if not completely out, was at least dying down. But it was close enough for Heather to catch a whiff of something like burning rubber from where she stood. Nick plunged forward and soon they lost it in the thick of the trees and brush.

They hurried along. Heather's heart began to pound, not just from the exercise. She'd never been at the scene of a crash site before, and all the horrid images that she'd ever seen on TV or in the newspapers flashed across her mind. Back at the ledge, when decisions had to be made, she'd been calm and logical. But now, on the brink of discovery and having had too much time to think about it, her imagination was beginning to run away with her.

Don't think about it too much, she kept telling herself, as she struggled to keep up with Nick. *Mind in the game. Mind in the moment.*

Another ridge rose before them. Nick hit it fast and hard and was at the top before Heather was even halfway.

"Hang on a second," he said, jogging down the line without waiting for them. "Just want to get a visual."

"Wait for us!" Heather shouted in response. She crested the ridge and without waiting for Jeff, who was a half-step behind, raced after him. The ridge wasn't long and there was a cleared rocky expanse only a few yards away. The burning rubber smell was stronger up here, so she knew they were close. Nick reached the open area before her and from the way his face fell when he looked outward, she knew it was bad.

Oh, God, Oh, God! She found herself praying. She reached the break in the tree-line, saying, "Nick, how bad is it-"

But she didn't finish. Nick grabbed her wrist and without warning pulled her down to the ground.

"Nick!"

"Quiet!" he whispered.

Jeff came up more slowly and did a double take when he saw them. "What are you…?"

"Shut *up* and get *down!*" Nick hissed. His face was white and rigid. "Get *down,* you idiot!"

It was then that Heather realized that his face wasn't pale from shock or horror. It was much worse than that. Her big brother, the boy who'd never been afraid of anything, was scared straight through.

Jeff, for once, did what he was told without commentary. He dropped and crawled on his knees and elbows to where they were crouched. Nick kept his hand on Heather's shoulder, restraining her from rising, and the brush in front of her kept her from seeing the crash site. Over the sound of the leaves in the breeze, she could hear faint metallic sounds, like someone lifting a squeaky car hood.

Someone was alive, then, working on the plane. But if that's all it was, why did Nick look like that? Then she remembered the bear scat and her heart went cold.

Jeff must have thought of the same thing.

"Is it the bear?" he whispered.

Nick waved his hand for quiet.

Jeff dropped his voice a few decibels and tried again. "I thought we were going to help them."

"Yeah..." Nick swallowed hard. His hand was gripping Heather's arm painfully now. "Yeah..."

Then he did something that really frightened Heather. He began to shrug off the backpack.

"Did either of you see the plane?" he whispered. "When it passed over us earlier, I mean?"

Jeff and Heather exchanged confused looks.

"No, we just said so," Heather whispered. "Sounded fast, though."

"Yeah," Jeff nodded. "Like an F-16."

"F-16? You saw it?" Nick sounded oddly hopeful, but he was gently, silently unzipping the front pocket of his backpack.

"I didn't see it, but it sounded like it. I used to go to the airbase with my father and *what is that?*"

Suddenly panicked, Jeff scrambled backwards. Nick, holding the pistol carefully pointed away, grabbed him by the shirt front and dragged him back.

"*Jeff*," he hissed. "I need you to keep calm, okay? Keep it cool!"

"Cool? *Cool?*" Jeff demanded. "We're in the middle of the forest, surrounded by bears and coyotes, about to go to the scene of plane crash, I almost died going over a cliff, you're pulling out guns and you want me to be *cool* about it?"

"It does seem to be asking a lot."

"Nick, what is going on?" Heather said. "What's over there?"

She started to get up, but Nick shoved her down before she could clear the bushes.

"Look, seriously, Jeff," he said. "I need you to stay calm and help me out, okay?"

For the first time since he'd met Jeff, Nick spoke without a trace of sarcasm. In fact, he looked downright desperate for Jeff's cooperation. Jeff and Heather exchanged looks again, before Jeff's eyes strayed back to the pistol.

"Of course," he said. "Cool as a cucumber."

"Is it a bear?" Heather asked.

Nick swallowed hard and shook his head.

"You know military planes?" he asked Jeff.

"Yeah, my father worked closely with the Air Force so I'm familiar with most standard issue…"

"Levinson…"

"The answer is yes," Jeff said hastily. "I do know them. Not to fly them, but to recognize them, I…"

"Then I need you to shut up and tell me what just landed over there," Nick snapped. "*And* do it without being seen, got it?"

Jeff opened his mouth, then closed it again and nodded. He crawled over to the line of bushes. Heather pushed Nick's hands away and followed him. As they got closer, the burning smell grew stronger as did a new sound: that of rushing water. Ferns and brush blocked their view and as Jeff was about to rise to peer over, Nick grabbed his wrist and pulled him around.

Making motions, he indicated *Quiet!* with a glare. Jeff nodded. Then both he and Heather rose up carefully.

They were overlooking a natural glade in the woods. A narrow brook ran along the perimeter several yards away, its sides edged with gravel and mud. The bank terminated in a small meadow of yellowing grass and browning weeds, bobbing and nodding in the autumn breeze. A furrow of freshly turned ground disturbed the natural beauty of the area, as did the ship that lay, scarred and cooling, with its nose in the stream.

To Heather's relief, there were no bodies or body parts scattered around the ship. In fact, it looked in remarkably good condition, considering what it had just gone through. Only the new scratches on its side and a few small pieces scattered here and there indicated that it had recently been through trauma.

On the whole, it was a rather tame looking plane crash site, with one large exception: the ship they were looking at was not an airplane at all. It was a space ship.

CHAPTER 7

Heather and Jeff stared.

There was no mistaking what the object was: a hermetically sealed space ship, made of metal cast in a dusty reddish hue, with unrecognizable lettering on the side. It was about the length of a bus, though broader and not as tall, and it had a smooth, graceful outline. The underbelly was buried under the dirt, but the nose, half submerged in the stream, bore the distinctive burn marks of atmospheric entry. There was no visible door or window. It lay there, in the afternoon sun, silent as a tomb.

Which, it may very well be, Heather thought, her heart hammering in her chest. *They could all be dead inside.*

There was no flag emblazoned on the side of the ship and its design was not American. Nor was it, by anything Heather knew, Russian or Chinese.

Whose could it be?

Nick tugged on her vest. She and Jeff dropped back down behind the bushes to face him. He looked nervous, his eyes darting from Jeff to Heather and back again. She was glad to see that the pistol was now tucked into his belt.

"Well?" Nick demanded in a whisper. "Is it ours?"

"It can't be," Heather said. "It doesn't have any of our markings on it."

"Then it's *got* to be one of theirs."

"Who's?"

"The Russians."

"But I thought their space program was dead."

"That was the story." Nick looked grim. "But who can believe anything they say? It's all propaganda. All I know is, if it *is* one of theirs, we've got to get help before they come to." He looked to Jeff, who was uncharacteristically quiet. "Well, space boy? Do you recognize it?"

Jeff hesitated, and then said, "I don't think it's Russian. The writing isn't in the Cyrillic alphabet. It's not Arabic either."

"Then it's ours?" Heather asked.

"Can't be," Nick said. "It just can't be."

"It's not," Jeff said.

"Well, if it isn't ours and it isn't from the USSR, whose *is* it?" Nick demanded. Though his voice remained soft, his pitch began to rise. "Who else has that kind of technology? Something so small and sleek and obviously fast – Who, China?"

"No, definitely not." Jeff shook his head. "They are light-years away from that kind of craft. So are we, as it happens."

"Then who?"

He hesitated again, and then looked at Nick with his eyebrows raised.

"I don't think it belongs to anybody *we* know," he said.

Nick stared at him, his mouth moving, but no sound coming out.

Aliens, Heather thought. *He thinks it's aliens.*

That was ridiculous. It was so ridiculous that she wanted to slap him for even thinking such a thing.

Instead, she said, "There's no window, no doors. Maybe it's not a passenger vehicle. Maybe it's, like, a new probe or something. You know, experimental."

That broke the spell holding Nick. He turned to her, sharp-eyed. "It'd still have the flag on it, wouldn't it?"

"Maybe not, if it's like, super-top-secret," Heather said.

Even she didn't believe that, but it was worth saying. Then, as the three of them knelt there, trying to figure out what to do, they heard it again — the sound of squeaking metal. It came from the clearing by the ship.

A cold feeling washed over her and the blood drained from Jeff's face. Nick's face, by contrast, grew harder.

"Someone's out there," Jeff whispered.

"Yeah," Nick responded. "Probably a passenger."

"We should look," Heather said. "The uniforms — we can tell who they are by the uniforms."

"They'll be armed," Jeff said. When both Millers looked at him, he amended this to, "Probably armed."

The squeaking sound changed. Now it was a grinding sound, like unbearable pressure being brought to bear on a metal body. Curiosity drove all three of them up from their crouching positions to peer over the bushes.

The ship was turning towards them now, the nose of the craft dripping mud and water. The rocks and gravel ground against the underbelly of the ship, screaming in protest as the heavy weight shifted over them. It moved steadily, smoothly, as though pushed by a much heavier machine. Yet there was nothing to be seen over the ship and no sound of a motor. It simply moved as though pushed.

"What on earth...?" Jeff muttered, but Nick waved for him to be silent.

The great ship moved and caught on something invisible. It shuddered for a moment, struggling against the obstacle, halfway out of the water. The dusty red color shone brilliantly in the afternoon sun and Heather thought she could detect a gradient in the color, something that caught the sun unlike smooth paint would.

The ship shuddered once more, and then lay still. There were scratching sounds, like something being pulled from under the ship. Something came sloshing through the water around the nose of the ship. Something taller than a man, with long legs and arms, dark gray scaly skin that glinted like a snake's, and a heavy head on a long neck that constantly moved. It was like nothing she had ever seen before, a dark, sinuous, looming thing, the stuff of nightmares.

Heather's breath caught in her throat and her hand jumped of its own accord to her mouth. She didn't scream, she *wouldn't* scream, but she desperately wanted to scream. She wanted to scream until she woke up and the nightmare disappeared in the light of the electric lamp and her mother's reassuring touch.

This can't be real. This can't be real. This is a nightmare – I'm asleep and I will wake up!

But she wasn't asleep, and she couldn't wake up. Stones dug through the denim to bite at her knees and horseflies, always present near bodies of water, buzzed around her head, looking for a place to land. She was awake and this was reality. And the three of them were stuck in the middle of nowhere, facing it.

The creature moved through the water with sure movements. Its oblong grey head moved to and fro, its large, liquid black eyes scanning, watching. Heather saw large hands with abnormally long digits and a jaw that was bulging and black. It was almost as tall as the ship and its long limbs moved, not so much with grace as with precision. The body was large and covered in some sort of black, leather-like armor. Across its chest was a belt of metallic objects that looked very much like weapons.

"Holy Christmas," Nick breathed and the sound made both Jeff and Heather jump and look at him. He glanced at Jeff in terror. "*You were right.*"

Jeff just swallowed and looked back towards the ship.

The creature moved along the side of the ship, clearly looking for the obstacle. The ship lay against a cluster of thin young birches. When the creature came upon them, it snagged them in the midsection, and tore them out, root and branch, as if they offered to more resistance than a daisy in a sidewalk. It flung the trees aside and continued forward, tearing through the resistant underbrush like a living weed-whacker.

As one, Nick and Heather lowered themselves back behind the bushes. As the initial shock ebbed away, Heather found herself feeling hollow and shaken, but oddly clear-headed. When she looked at Nick, she saw that he was feeling the same.

"What do we do?" she whispered.

Nick shook his head, then hesitated, and looked back the way they'd come. "We have to get back to the truck. We have to warn them."

"The rangers?"

"Everyone," he said grimly. He turned to her, his blue eyes wide with disbelief. "Heather, we've been *invaded.*"

Part Two:
THE ENCOUNTER

CHAPTER 8

*I*nvaded.

The word hung in the air like the sword of Damocles. Even as he said it, Nick could hardly believe it. It was something sci-fi stories always predicted, something that military heads always thought possible, though in human form. It was something that Nick had always, in a remote way, feared and expected, the true reason why he wanted to join the Marines. But that it was here and now, when they were so unprepared, seemed unfair.

I'm not ready. Lord, I'm not ready…

"Such a small ship," Heather whispered. When Nick looked at her, her eyes were huge and her face white. She gestured helplessly, like a child. "For an invasion, I mean."

"It could be an exploratory vessel," Jeff whispered. "Or a scout ship."

Of course – a scout ship. That had to be it. Nick shook his head to clear it, but shock was hard to shake. This was impossible. Yet it was happening.

Focus on the here and now.

First things first, and the first thing was keeping Heather and Jeff safe. They were just kids and under his protection. Somehow, he had to get them out of the woods and back to safety, wherever that was now. Next, they had to warn the authorities. Who knew how many more of these ships had already landed or what their real purpose was. Hopefully Jeff was right about this being a scout ship, not the first wave of an assault. The military had to be informed, and the local authorities. Mom and Dad had to be told – they weren't that far away, relaxing, partying with the family…

The thought of his family, sitting unaware in the remote resort made Nick's heart pound in fear. There could be more of these ships, more of these creatures, landing all across the countryside, ready to…

Focus, Miller. One task at a time.

Jeff dropped next to them, his face a mask of concentration. "Their sensors must not be very good," he said. "If this were Star Trek, they'd have picked up on our life forms immediately."

Fear gave way to fury. Nick turned on Jeff. "This *isn't* Star Trek!" he shouted in a whisper. "This is real life and we're in real trouble. We've got to get out of here before we are…"

A sound, something like a cross between a whistle and a bird's chirrup, stopped him mid-sentence. It came from behind them and once again, they got up to peer over the bushes.

The alien being had cleared most of the underbrush from around the ship, leaving its metallic sides glinting in the sun. As it moved back to the front of the ship, it looked around again, the powerful jaw working. The three instantly dropped back down. They waited, tense, listening – had they been seen?

Heather looked at Jeff. He gave her a half-hearted reassuring smile and Nick was reminded, once again, of how young and helpless they were.

Keep your head or they will lose theirs.

Nick slowly rose again, peering carefully over the bushes. The other two joined him after a moment of hesitation.

The alien was now at the tip of the ship, grasping the nose with its two wide hands. The chirruping sound grew louder and now he could see that the sounds were synced up with the jaw-muscle work. The alien was speaking – but to whom?

As if in answer to his unspoken question, a patch on the side of the ship began to shimmer, like jello fresh from a mold. Through this shimmer, though no door opened and the wall never moved, another alien appeared. It was also gray with a black jaw, but it was easily half the size of the first alien, and it had a jagged patch along the side of its head, like a scar or the remains of a burn. It ambled over to the first alien, chirruping in its turn.

Now Heather gave Nick a panicky look. The alien ship needed no doors – which meant the entire ship could be one great big window, with untold eyes watching them. Nick fought the urge to drop and crawl away. But the very fact that the aliens were not reacting to their presence meant they had not been seen… yet.

The larger of the two aliens grunted twice at the smaller one before wrapping its large hands around the nose of the ship. Then it *lifted* the ship, pulling it until it was completely on dry land. When it stepped back, it in no way acted winded or as if this were any sort of real effort. It merely directed the scarred alien to go around the other side, presumably to do some work there.

Nick's heart was hammering and his grip on the pistol grew slick with perspiration. The alien was that much stronger than them and, judging from the long legs, probably able to out run them as well. If they were armed as well as the tech on their ship would suggest, the humans were in far greater danger than he'd first supposed. And that first supposition had been bad enough to start with.

The two aliens disappeared around the side of the ship and the three humans dropped back behind the bushes.

"Holy cow," Heather whispered. "How strong *are* they?"

"Judging from the impression in the gravel," Jeff mused. "That ship is no paper boat."

"Yah think?" Nick growled.

"We've got to get out of here," Heather said. "They're bound to find us if we wait."

"They don't seem very nervous," Jeff said.

"Why should they be?" Nick demanded. "They're in the middle of nowhere and obviously physically superior to all of us. *They've* got nothing to worry about." He pulled the pistol out again and indicated the woods through which they'd come. "Come on, Heather's right. We've got to make tracks and *quietly*."

Heather nodded, but Jeff put a restraining hand on her arm.

"We can't just leave," he said. "What are we going to tell the authorities?"

"We tell them what we saw," Nick said. "Just exactly what we saw."

"Do that and they'll think you're crazy. People report little green men all the time. No one believes them. You yourself told me I was crazy for thinking amoebas might exist on another planet."

"Look, if I apologize and let you say 'I told you so', will you get moving? We don't have a lot of time. The sun will be down in a few hours and I don't want to be stuck in the woods with those things."

"But he's right, Nick." Heather was shaking, her teeth rattling with tension, but her words were steady. "No one is going to believe us."

"Well, what *else* can we do?" Nick growled. "Stay here? Fight them barehanded?"

"We need proof," Jeff said.

Nick threw his hands up. "Oh, fine, great idea! I'll sneak over and get a skin sample from one of them or tag the small one before we release them back into the wild. Use your heads!"

"Use *yours*," Heather snapped.

"Shut up!"

"You shut up!"

"I was more thinking," Jeff broke in suddenly, shifting so that his body was between them, "that we could bring back photographic evidence." He held up the camera.

Heather looked at Nick, who flushed and shuffled his feet.

Shoot.

They were right, of course. The idea of not being believed had never occurred to Nick, but then again, he wasn't the type who generally believed in hare-brained things like alien invasions. Though every fiber in his being screamed to get the kids out of there before they were spotted, escaping now would be pointless if he couldn't save them from the invasion later. To save the others, they needed to bring back proof – and Jeff had the only means.

"Okay," he muttered. "Okay, fine. Can you take it without them seeing you?"

"Sure. They do it in the wild with apes all the time."

Nick gritted his teeth, forcing down frustration born of fear. "Then let's do it and be quiet, for God's sake."

Jeff nodded and crept back to the bushes. He craned his neck to peer over. "They're still on the other side."

"Then take a picture of the ship," Nick said.

Jeff did, snapping three quick shots before crouching back down. "Got it."

"Let's go."

"It's no good without the aliens. As far as NASA or National Security is concerned, it's just a big weird ship."

Nick swore under his breath, but Jeff was right again. Heather went to crouch at Jeff's side, wrapping her arms around herself. Nick kept his hand on the pistol and his eye on the woods, watching for movement, praying that whatever these things were, they weren't impervious to lead.

They waited, listening for the chirruping sounds that would indicate the aliens' return.

Jeff wiped his forehead with his sleeve. "Is it hot or is it just me?"

It wasn't hot, but Nick didn't feel the need to point this out. All around them, the forest seemed to roar with movement. Leaves tore into each other and pinecones dropped with thunderous weight. Squirrels and chipmunks running through the crisp bedding sounded four times louder than they actually were. But there was no sound from the ship nor the aliens behind it. The natural noises of the woods seemed amplified, as if in a conspiracy to cover the invaders.

Nick glanced at his companions. Heather was white, her jaw taut with strain. Jeff seemed calmer now that he had a task to perform. Nick was willing to bet that this calm would dissipate the moment he snapped the picture.

Maybe we should go while they're occupied. But reason triumphed again. Jeff *was* right: without a picture, no one would believe them and valuable time, time that might be counted in human lives, would be lost.

A chirruping sound, small and almost lost in the white noise of the mountainside, alerted them. It was close and the response was even closer. There was the sound of scraping metal, too. The aliens had returned to the other side of the ship.

Nick glanced at Jeff, who swallowed hard. He half rose, but Nick pulled him back down. If anyone was going to take the first risk, it would be Nick, not the kids in his care. He took a breath and carefully rose, peering over the brush.

The little glade was dappled with light and shadow. The brisk breeze was tugging small clouds across the million-acre sky. Trees and tall stalks of grass bobbed and waved as the birds, who had been quiet, took up their chorus again. Nature was returning to normal, a new normal that included an orange-red space ship occupied by gray and black alien beings.

The aliens were working on the ship, unaware of their human audience. Nick waved for Jeff to join him. Before Jeff could move, however, Heather reached out and squeezed his hand. He looked surprised – but he squeezed back. Heather smiled.

Oh, jeez...

Now was most definitely *not* the time for a moment.

"Levinson!" Nick hissed.

Jeff released her hand and rose, camera at the ready. Heather got up with him and carefully, slowly, peered up over the brush.

The aliens were dragging two long, heavy rods which they dropped carelessly on the ground. The first alien crouched by the front of the ship and placed its wide hands on the nose. It leaned in, listening to the interior.

The scarred alien watched it for a moment, then turned and began to walk towards the woods at the base of the ship. It walked casually, but its head never stopped moving, swinging side to side, as though watching. Its hands, too, remained on its heavy belt, where an array of objects, probably weapons, though different in size and shape from the first alien's, hung.

A sentry, Nick thought. *So they are nervous after all...*

It was surprising how little comfort that offered.

Jeff was staring, mesmerized by the sight. He jolted when Nick nudged him, as though he just remembered the camera. He lifted it to his eyes, but hesitated and looked at Nick. Suddenly, Nick understood: the sound of the shutter wasn't very loud, but who knew how well the aliens could hear?

The scarred alien, whom Nick decided was the Sentry, was at the tree line now, peering into it while chirruping softly. The mechanical alien, or the Mechanic, moved from the nose of the ship and back to the long rods. Its back was to them. The Sentry was facing south, away from them, and the breeze had picked up again, the leaves rustling loudly overhead. There was no better time to take the picture.

Jeff's finger lowered and gently pressed. The *click* sounded like a ricochet and Nick's heart caught. But nothing happened. Neither alien even twitched. He glanced at Jeff and saw his face drop with relief.

They'd done it. They'd gotten photographic proof.

Now to get these two out of here...

Nick gestured *Let's go,* but Jeff shook his head. He'd only gotten the one alien. He wanted a picture of both. He adjusted his lens and leaned in.

Click.

Still no reaction. The Mechanic worked, the Sentry chirruped into the woods, the breeze shifted the clouds around, the birds responded to each other's call. All was right with the world.

Jeff adjusted his lens and leaned in for one more.

The clouds shifted and a shadow fell across him. The Sentry turned its head. Nick moved to stop Jeff, but it was too late.

Click.

The automatic flash seared through the afternoon light like a thunderclap on a still August day. The Sentry squealed, whipping about, reaching for one of the dull metallic objects that hung from its belt. The Mechanic, who was closer and bigger, dropped the rods and peered up at the bluff where the three humans stood, frozen in terror. Its hand, too, reached for one of the items on its belt, but it did not pull it out – the hand lay there, grasping the weapon as the enormous black eyes scanned the surroundings.

The three humans stood frozen, rooted to the ground in a common, elemental fear.

Nick thought, *This is it. This where we die.*

No one moved. No one even breathed. For a long, agonizing minute, the two alien beings stared at the three humans and the fate of all five quivered in the balance. Then the Sentry chirruped, only to be cut off by an impatient hand gesture from the Mechanic. The Mechanic stepped forward, a long, predatory step that seemed even more threatening than the weapons on its belt. Still it scanned. It did not draw a weapon.

It's like it's not seeing us, Nick thought. *But how can it not?*

He glanced at Jeff. At his slight movement, the Sentry sounded an alarm and Nick froze. The Mechanic drew a weapon and took another step forward, its head moving like a hawk in search of rodents. The Sentry moved too, the weapon held carefully in its hand. Then the Mechanic's jaw moved and a sound, like that of wild eagle in triumph, erupted from him, piercing the afternoon calm.

It's trying to startle us, he realized. *To get us to move. It needs us to move. If we can just stand still, maybe…*

He didn't get a chance to finish that thought. A responding chirrup exploded from the woods just a few yards to Heather's right. Before Nick could do anything, she screamed, jumped, and turned.

The trees bent and swayed and a body emerged, tall and gray, with a heavy belt around its waist and red stains down its chest and shoulders. A deer, limp and empty-eyed, dangled from around its neck, looking small as a fox caplet on the enormous alien shoulders.

There were three aliens, not two. And this particular alien had its weapon drawn.

Nick stood frozen, his body and mind incapable of thought or movement. They were about to be killed. All of them. Dead.

The alien hunter took a step forward, looming over Heather, chirruping in triumph. Then it reached for her.

CHAPTER 9

Heather couldn't breathe. The alien loomed closer, its shadow blocking the light of the dying sun, its body so close she could smell the tangy scent of fresh blood and something saline, and feel the heat emanating from the enormous body. The wheezing warmth of its breath stroked her face. Terror rooted her to the ground and though her mouth hung open, she couldn't speak or scream.

I'm going to die…

"Heather!"

She couldn't identify the voice or the hand that seized her wrist and yanked her out from under the looming threat. One minute she was rooted in place, the next she was running, trying frantically to keep up with the boys. Jeff was pulling her, Nick shoving them past him so he could take up the rear, the pistol tight in his hand. The alien roared in tinny frustration and when Heather glanced behind, she saw the hunter shrug the deer from its shoulders as it prepared to chase after them. Answering calls rang out from the clearing below.

"Go, go, *go!*" Nick shouted, shoving her.

They raced across the narrow top of the ridge and down the steep side. Fallen branches and low bushes reached to entangle their ankles. One took Jeff down and he landed spread-eagle on the hard-packed ground.

Heather stopped to help, but Nick shoved her again. "*Move it!*"

She stumbled forward, looking behind. The hunter had cleared the ridge and stood at the edge, getting its bearings. It held the deer limp in one hand. When it saw the boys, Nick tugging Jeff to his feet, it roared again. Then it lifted the animal by the two hind legs, whipped it over head, and threw it.

"Nick!" Heather screamed.

He saw it in time to duck and roll. Jeff duplicated the action in the opposite direction. The heavy carcass smashed into the ground between them with a sickening crunch, limbs and head flopping loosely. Jeff's roll landed him at Heather's feet. She reached down to pull him up, keeping her eye on the ridge. The hunter turned to cry over its shoulder. Then it looked directly at Heather.

Jeff was saying, "…threw it like it weighed nothing…" but Heather wasn't paying attention. She was watching the hunter as it stepped backwards, preparing to spring.

"Jeff…"

The hunter leapt, clearing yards, arms and fingers extended; for the first time, Heather saw the claws. The hunter landed only inches away from the carcass, the ground shaking with its landing. On the ridge behind, the Mechanic appeared, armed and calling.

Nick gained his feet, pistol in still in hand, blood from the carcass spattered across his face.

"*Run!*" he shouted and raised the gun.

Heather grabbed Jeff's arm and pulled him into the dense woods behind them. Shadows covered them and the sound of a pistol shot brought Heather to a halt. The alien's scream made her whip around. "Nick!"

There was a crashing sound and Nick appeared, wild-eyed. Behind him came the sound of splintering wood.

"Go go *go!*" he shouted.

They ran, Nick in the lead, holding the pistol, Jeff and Heather neck-and-neck behind him. Nick plowed through

UNIVERSAL THREAT

bushes and leapt over fallen tree trunks, pausing only long enough to look behind. Heather didn't allow herself the luxury. She ran, slipping on the soft forest bedding, heart pounding. The dense woods began to thin out as they reached level ground and the heavy thudding footsteps drew nearer. Then they stumbled into an open area and Nick stopped, looking around frantically.

Heather's sides were screaming in pain and she gasped for breath. Jeff was almost as bad, but he looked behind her.

"They're getting closer," he said.

"No kidding." Nick looked right, where the level land gave way to mountain side, then left, where the mountain wall climbed up. He pointed right. "There. Come on!"

He took off again and Jeff and Heather followed. Just beyond a few trees, a grouping of granite boulders lay like a neglected pile of children's toys. Nick headed straight towards it, gaining speed as he went.

"Come on, come on!"

Heather's legs felt ready to give way. The thrashing sound of the alien's approach grew louder and closer behind them. Nick was at the boulders, gesturing. Jeff was a few paces in front, turning to silently urge her on. The thrashing sounds grew so close she could almost hear the wheezy sound of the alien's breath. Now Jeff was climbing the rocks and Nick was reaching for her, one hand out, the other clutching the pistol. From somewhere behind her, wood snapped, and she thought, *It's here, it's here, I'm dead...*

But then Nick's hand grasped hers and she was pulled up.

"Get down, get down!" Nick hissed.

The grouping of boulders was the remains of a single one large one that had been split when a second fell on it years ago. The shards, still rough edged and glistening with moisture, created crevasses just large enough for their slender bodies to hide in. She slipped down into one. Jeff wriggled into another. Nick took one last look around, then, as the trees in front of

68

him exploded in a shower of twigs and branches, he dove down into the shadowy crevasses and wiggled into the shadows.

Outside, just yards from where they were hiding, the alien emerged from the woods.

Heather hunkered down as low as she could go. The crevasse she'd wedged herself into narrowed towards the ground and she pushed downward until she was very nearly stuck. The rocks were cool to the touch and slippery with moss. Close by her ear, something skittered away, but for once she was too afraid of something larger to yield to her usual arachnophobia. She could hear Jeff's noisy breath, but she couldn't see him. All she could see was the sky overhead and Nick's hand a short distance away, knuckles white against the dark pistol grip.

Heavy, thudding footsteps drew nearer. Heather shoved her fist into her mouth to stop from crying out.

Please don't have a scanning thing. Please, please, please don't have a scanning thing...

The sky overhead darkened with the outline of the head. It was leaning *over* them. The stones trembled under the weight of the beast as the alien clambered up with a grunt. A foot appeared inches from Heather's face, oblong toes gripping the edge tightly, short, razor like claws tapping the rock with ominous clicks. High above her head, something in the alien's hand buzzed like a welding tool and intermittent light dazzled her eyes.

The weapon... it has a weapon.

Heather lay still, not breathing, not moving, not daring to blink. The alien shifted its stance and the boulders shifted in response. The rock in front of Heather twisted until it was nearly touching her chest. She gasped and shoved her hands in front of her in response, only just stopping herself from screaming. But the gasp was loud enough, and the alien's head swung around at the sound.

Heather froze. The alien froze. Overhead, a bird cried out. Below, Heather's heart thudded so hard she was certain the alien could hear it. Tears ran down her face, tickling her chin.

Oh God, oh God, please, not Nick, not Jeff, please, please, please...

The hunter leaned forward, lowering its head and listening. Then, abruptly, it straightened and in one swift movement, leapt off the rocks. Heather could feel the reverberation of its landing on the ground and then the heavy steps moved off swiftly.

Nothing was left behind but silence.

CHAPTER 10

Tears coursed freely down Heather's cheeks. She buried her face in her arm as tremors ran the length of her body. She could hear Nick grunting as he wriggled out of his hiding place to take a look. Someone nudged her shoulder and Heather raised her face to the light. Jeff leaned against the stone above her, offering a hand up. Nick was perched on the top of the rocks, looking both ways. He glanced down at her and gestured: *Quickly.*

Jeff took her hand and she wriggled and twisted. The rocks had shifted under the alien's weight, closing her in and making it hard to move. Jeff pulled, but she made little progress until Nick came down and grabbed her other hand. She emerged, unharmed but still crying. She fell back against one of the stones and pressed her hands to her eyes, shaking under the weight of the silent sobs.

A hand grasped her shoulder.

"Heather," Nick said, low and close. "Come on. Heather, we've got to go, all right?"

She nodded, drawing in deep, shaky breaths. In the distance, they heard the calling chirrup of one of the *things.* Leaves rustled in the breeze. Nick crouched in front of her, looking around cautiously. Jeff was inexplicably patting down his own pockets, as though looking for a pencil.

"Nick," he whispered.

"Later," Nick said. He stood upright and looked around, orienting himself. He gestured back the way they had come. "There's a stream back that way," he said. "It's in a ravine. If we follow up, it'll lead us back to the trail."

"Upstream," Jeff said, nodding. "Got it." He looked around nervously, rubbing his hands together.

Heather gulped back her panic. "They- They'll be back, won't they?"

Nick looked at Jeff and nodded. "Yeah. And we'd better not be here when they do."

"Did you see how they moved," Jeff said thoughtfully. "Fast, strong, almost like panthers, but stronger and smarter. And their eyes; it almost seemed like they could…"

"Dude, not the time," Nick interrupted. He pointed. "The stream is in that direction. Whatever happens, find it, follow it upwards, and you'll be back on the trail. Got it?"

"Got it," Heather and Jeff chimed in together.

"The aliens are bigger than us and can't maneuver through the trees as quickly," he went on. "With their strength, it didn't hold them up much, but it's a slight advantage, so *if* something comes at us again, head to the densest part of the forest. You'll buy yourself some time to run."

"Also their eyes," Jeff said.

"What about them, Levinson?"

"They only really seemed to pick up on movement," he said. "Like birds, you know? Some raptors can't see unless their prey is moving."

Nick and Heather exchanged glances. "You thought so, too?" Nick asked.

Jeff shrugged. "We'd have to do some experimentation to be sure, but…"

"*That* ain't happening," Nick cut him off. "We're moving right now."

He looked at Heather and she nodded, pushing herself up on to her feet.

Nick tucked the pistol into his waistband and hopped over the stones. "Come on, guys, let's go."

"There's just one thing," Jeff said, only to be brutally cut off by, "Not *now*, Space Boy!"

Heather wiped her nose one last time, and followed, landing easily on the flat ground below. She steadied herself, noting a lot more branches on the ground than had been there before.

She waited as Jeff swung his legs over. Nick moved forward cautiously, keeping in the shadows of the trees as he scanned the forests.

Heather looked back at Jeff and gestured. *Come on!*

Jeff hesitated, and then pushed himself off the rock. He hit the ground hard, rolling awkwardly.

"Ouch!" he said as Heather went to give him a hand up.

Nick whipped around and glared.

"Will you two keep quiet!" he growled.

"Why are we going that way?" Jeff asked, indicated the path through which the alien had come.

"Because, genius, the alien went *that* way." Nick pointed back towards behind the rocks that they'd been hiding in. "And the stream is this way, so let's *move!*"

He ran on ahead. Heather pulled Jeff to his feet and made sure he was fine before turning to follow Nick. He moved swiftly, following the trail by which they'd come, moving his head back and forth in watch. Jeff soon caught up with her and they moved as quietly as possible, picking their way carefully through the underbrush.

A fresh path had been cut through the woods. Branches from ground-level to higher than Heather's head had been torn away or broken in the alien's mad dash to find them. The air was heavy with a burning scent, mingling with that of freshly cut wood and free flowing sap.

Good grief, how strong is that thing?

Judging from the sick look on Nick's face, he was thinking the same thing.

Heather was still musing on this, listening with all her might for sounds of an approach, when Jeff raced up next to her, holding a stout tree branch. He grabbed her arm to pull her around.

"Heather, look at this!" he said and handed it to her.

The wood was warm, warmer than a fallen branch in October ought to be, and it hadn't been torn or broken. The end was sheer, as though someone had hacked the three-inch thick branch from the tree with one smooth blow. But no knife had done it. The end was scorched.

She looked at Jeff.

He looked grim. "Laser."

The welding sound – that weapon!

She'd been right – those things in their belts hadn't been tools, but weapons. Laser weapons.

We've got to get out of here. We've got to tell them, tell everyone, before it's too late. Thank goodness we have the...

Then realization struck her hard. She looked at Jeff again. He was still in front of her, his vest open, polo shirt stained and dirty from the tumble he'd taken earlier. His hands were empty and there was nothing around his neck.

"Where's your camera?" she demanded.

He gestured back towards the crash site.

Oh no!

No pictures, no proof. And now she knew they had laser capabilities.

Nick was several yards ahead, striding forward, head bent over his compass, the backpack low on his back. He didn't know. He was intent on getting them home, on getting *her* home safely.

Heather opened her mouth to call to him, thought better of it and ran instead. Jeff raced after her. Their careless steps on the new bedding sounded loud under the tall pines.

Nick whipped around, furious.

"Will you two keep - !"

"Nick, we-"

She was cut off.

The Mechanic burst out of the trees between them barely a yard in front of Heather, roaring and furious. It struck the ground hard, kicking up dirt and brush. Dirt hit Heather and she screamed, throwing her hands up, scrambling to stop. She heard Nick shout and then Jeff's arm caught her around the waist, stopping her from falling.

"*Freeze!*" he shouted. Heather could feel his warmth and the thudding of his heart against hers.

The Mechanic scrambled to its feet in the loosened bedding, its mottled green and brown skin shifting back into to the familiar gray and black. Its hands were empty, for the moment and the claws showed clearly in the dappled sunlight. It swayed from one side to the other, then, even though they hadn't moved, it swung around on Heather and Jeff. One hand reached for his belt.

Oh God, oh God...

"Hey, *hey!!*"

Nick's voice filled the clearing.

The creature snapped around. Nick had advanced recklessly and was leveling the pistol for a shot, but he didn't have time to fire. A gray hand flashed and Nick sailed backwards through the air, landing on his back. The pistol skittered several yards away and Nick, after an initial moan, lay still.

Heather cried out in anger and tore out of Jeff's arms. Realizing she still held the branch, she ran at the Mechanic, swinging.

"No, Heather, *no!*"

She swung, using every ounce of muscle and skill honed from hours in the soft ball field. She made contact so hard her hands stung, her palms tingled, and the branch shattered on the bony shoulders of the being. A screech of something that might have been pain hit her as hard in the ears as the blow to her stomach knocked the breath out of her.

She landed a few feet away. A fireworks display of darkness and color clouded her vision. She rolled instinctively to one side. Nick was shouting, Jeff was shouting. She got up on-to her knees and shook her vision clear.

Jeff was in front of her, hurling rocks at the creature, shouting to keep its attention. Across the way, Nick scrambled for his pistol. The creature was in the middle, roaring in anger, hands up in front of its face. It wasn't reaching for its weaponry. It just stood there, taking the blows. But why?

"Nick!" she screamed. "They have weapons!"

"Of course they do!" was his response.

The ground was shaking then, but it wasn't from the Mechanic's stumblings. It came from behind Jeff.

Heather hopped to her feet and turned just as the branches from the trees behind Jeff sheared away against a crescendo of chirrups.

The Hunter had returned to the scene.

Only then did the Mechanic reach for its weapons.

"Jeff, behind you!"

Jeff turned and saw the Hunter. The stones fell from his hands.

The Hunter took one long bounding leap forward and landed inches from Jeff's face, brandishing the weapon that coughed in its hand.

A shot rang out. The Mechanic roared and staggered. The Hunter stopped and looked up. Heather caught a glimpse of Nick, running, drawing the attention of the creatures.

"*Heather, get to the stream!*" he screamed and fired again.

Heather was already running. She darted between the two aliens, grabbed Jeff's hand and lunged into the thick brush beyond, dragging him along with them.

The creature was right behind.

CHAPTER 11

The branches closed in behind Heather and Jeff, concealing them from sight. Nick waited until he could no longer see them turning before roaring as loud as he could. Two alien heads swung in his direction, just as he planned. The Mechanic was favoring an arm, but Nick didn't stop to shoot again. He shouted, just to be sure he had their attention – and then he turned tail and ran.

Follow me, follow me, for God's sake, follow me!

He shot a look over his shoulder. The Mechanic, roaring in pain and clutching the shoulder that Nick had shot, stepped aside to allow the Hunter to pass. The Hunter was gaining ground, weapon activated in hand, head and eyes unswerving. It was coming to kill Nick.

Which was just what he wanted.

Nick veered sharply left, into the densest of the forest and in the opposite direction of the stream. His heavy boots bit the ground, their sure grip making up for their weight. He had to keep upright and moving. He had to buy Jeff and Heather time.

I promised you, Dad, and she will get home safely…

The trees behind him began to buck and weave, like a forest in the middle of a nor'easter. The ground reverberated with heavy footsteps. The savage whine of the weapon as it sliced through branches kept him moving forward. But even with the branches slowing it down, that alien made good time.

Lasers – they have fricking lasers!

Which made it all the more imperative that Heather and Jeff escape. Not simply because Heather was his sister, but also because of Jeff's camera.

Lasers! Space Boy's friggin' fantasies are coming true.

Nick chose his path like an obstacle course, jumping over falling logs, dodging through trees, ducking under branches, looking for somewhere to hide. The alien was moving fast, but despite its strength and the use of the lasers, it was still lagging, giving Nick much needed time to make tracks.

Running was something that came easily to Nick, thanks to his daily practice in preparation for Marine Corps training. But he couldn't keep up the mad pace indefinitely. He looked wildly about as he ran, seeking a hiding spot to catch his breath.

Though if Jeff is right, all I need to do is stand still.

Like that was going to happen. Nick wasn't up to any experimentation.

The terrain was doing one of its rapid shifts, the relatively level ground shifting into an uphill climb, requiring more than just fleet feet. He shoved the pistol back into his waistband and threw himself at the incline. His boots slipped on soft earth, digging for purchase, overturning wet leaves to expose the dark earth underneath. He just managed to make it up the top when the Hunter appeared in a gap in the trees. It spotted him and bounded up the mountain side.

Nick swore and ran. The heavy backpack bounced on his back, almost throwing him off balance when he ran too close to the edge. A curve in the landscape came up and he threw himself down the embankment, half-running, half-sliding down the hill. He stumbled at the bottom of the incline, eyes sharp for any means of escape.

Give me something, give me something!

The creature emerged from the tree cover on the hill above him and screamed in triumph. Nick tore through the bushes and trees along the edge of the incline, feeling as much as hearing the thud when the creature jumped. Then he saw it – a hole in the side of the hill. The sound of splintering wood propelled him forward. He gained the entrance just as the first glimpse of the laser poked through the trees, and threw himself in.

Nick slammed his shoulder into the cave wall and scrambled to pull his feet inside. Then he waited, listening, catching his breath. The sudden darkness blinded him. The cave was small and close, only just tall enough for him to curl up in it. There was a heavy smell and the ground was slick underneath. Weeds rimming the entrance provided extra cover, so Nick drew himself up so that he could see out.

Outside, the heavy thuds grew nearer as the Hunter charged through the thicket, weapon in hand. It swung its heavy head around, scanning the area, listening in its turn.

Nick's breath was coming out in gasps, gasps he tried hard to suppress. Jeff had said they could only see movement. He hadn't mentioned whether or not the aliens had superior hearing and Nick wasn't about to become a test case for them.

The alien looked around and began to move forward.

It was then that Nick heard a new sound: a feral, low growling, so close it was practically in his ear.

Nick turned. A furred, pointed face snarled inches away from his own, teeth bared and hackles erect.

Shoot!

Nick threw himself backward and out of the cave. The coyote followed, barking and snapping at Nick's leg. Nick shouted back and yanked the leg away, pedaling backwards on his hands. His right hand fell on a rock. He threw it and nailed the coyote in the chest. The coyote flinched, pausing a moment in its rush to recover. Nick gained his feet, the coyote leapt. It was too close to miss. Nick threw up his hands, bracing for an impact – which never came.

From out of nowhere, a gray hand swatted the coyote away like an insect.

The Hunter had returned.

Nick didn't even think about pulling the pistol. He ran. The coyote howled, the Hunter screeched in reply and when Nick glanced back, it was just in time to see the coyote leap into the path of the Hunter's laser blade.

Its body rolled one way, it's head another.

Grunting in satisfaction, the Hunter swung around, ready for its next victim.

Shoot, shoot, shoot!

CHAPTER 12

They were running. Branches scraped at their faces while lower bushes and slippery pine needles threatened their balance. Heather's side was screaming in pain and her legs felt like they were filled with wet sand, yet she wouldn't have stopped had Jeff not pulled her to a halt.

"Wait, wait, wait," he wheezed.

Heather ground to a halt and wiped her slick forehead. Sweat trickled down her sides and her head pounded with a thirst-induced ached.

Jeff wasn't any better. He bent over at the waist, drawing in long breaths like a parched man lapping up water. He was pale and his longs limbs shook, whether from effort or from nerves, it was impossible to tell.

Around them, the woods seemed as normal. The leaves danced in the breeze and squirrels scattered on their approach. Heather couldn't stand still. She prowled nervously around Jeff, her eyes frantically scanning their surroundings. She couldn't see anything alarming, of course, but that was no comfort. Foremost on her mind was the memory of the green/brown alien returning to gray.

They can camouflage. They could be anywhere. Oh, God, they could be here!

"We can't wait," she said. "We have to meet Nick at the stream." When Jeff didn't seem prone to move, she grabbed his arm and tried to drag him. "Jeff, come *on!*"

"Nick…" he wheezed.

Her heart clutched, but she shook her head. "The stream," she said. "He'll be waiting for us."

Nick had to be there. Any other alternative was impossible to think about. When Jeff still hesitated, she shook him. "We have got to *go!*"

He reluctantly nodded. She released his arm and turned back the direction they'd been heading. It was then that she realized that she really didn't know which way the stream was. She looked up at the sky, but her view of the sun was partially obscured by the pines and the looming summit of Mount Stark. Not that she was all *that* sure of the directional – Nick had always been the expert there.

"Which way?" Jeff asked.

She looked around, found a mountain slope, and pointed. "That way," she said, with more confidence than she felt.

"All right." Jeff pulled a stout branch from under a pile of leaves and needles. It was birch, fairly fresh, with a few twigs growing off the side of it.

"Good idea," she said, wishing she'd thought of it.

"No reason to think we won't be followed," he replied. He pulled at the twigs, indicating that Heather should start.

Why did you have to say that?

They set off.

The slope was steeper here and the trees close together. They followed the curve of the mountain, carefully making their way down. The ground was orange and brown with fallen pine needles, the carpet broken here and there by jagged stones and rotting stumps. All around them, the trees rustled, a white noise that covered their movements, but also blinded them to the movements of anything else.

Nick could be a yard from me in any direction, Heather thought, trying to keep her hopes up.

There hadn't been another pistol shot which could mean anything. She decided not to dwell on any other possibility than the one that had Nick waiting for them by the stream.

Now the terrain dropped sharply. Pines clung to steep sides of the mountain, but the bushes disappeared. From far below, the cheerful rushing sounds of water rose above the white noise.

Jeff came up behind her, breathing on her neck.

"The stream," he said. "We made it."

"Yes," she answered shortly. She scanned the hillside and listened, but there was no sound or sign that anyone else was present.

"Should we go down?" Jeff asked.

"Yeah…" She looked around and saw where the earth had formed into a natural path, narrow and twisting and winding downhill. "Let's follow that way."

"Right." He sounded much more cheerful. "Do you see Nick?"

"Not yet."

"Right."

He didn't say anymore. He followed her as she threaded her way through the trees, wondering what she should do if she should get to the stream and Nick didn't show. She couldn't leave him behind – but what would Jeff do?

As if on cue, Jeff grabbed her arm and pulled her to sharp halt.

"Did you hear that?" he asked.

They listened. Overhead, birds called and a woodpecker chopped. Leaves rustled and the stream chuckled. And just underneath all these sounds, something moved through the woods, softly, cautiously.

Her breath caught.

"Nick?" she whispered.

Jeff listened for a moment, and then shook his head. "I don't know." He looked around and pointed to a clump of young trees. "Come on."

They ran, their feet sliding on the slippery bedding. The trees were young but, thankfully, still heavy with leaves, creating a sort of wooden cave just large enough for Jeff and Heather to slip into. Heather went in first, Jeff following after, taking the stick with him. Then they waited, trying not to breathe too loudly, listening and watching.

Heather tried to calm her head and her heart. The scent of pine and soil was heavy in the air, hopefully covering their own scent. She wasn't altogether sure how good the aliens' sense of smell was, but better to err on the side of caution.

Nothing happened.

Their breathing slowed and her heart rate lowered, though her nerves remained as taut as ever. She became keenly aware of other details: the rich orange of the leaves dancing in the breeze, the feel of the stones beneath her knees, the crinkling sounds of Jeff's jacket, the way his arm kept brushing up against her own. A strong impulse to wrap her arms around him swept over her, but she kept her hands to herself. Even the slightest sound might give them away.

Jeff's jacket creaked as he shifted, peering around the trunks of the trees.

"I think it's gone," he whispered.

"Good," Heather muttered through chattering teeth. "Good."

"Now what do we do?"

She wanted to stay where she was. She wanted to curl up in a little ball, pull her jacket over her head, and wait until the rescue party found her. She wanted to know that Nick was all right. She wanted to be home right now, next to Great Aunt Dora, listening to her surgery story for the millionth time.

But none of these could happen. Not unless she did something.

"We have to get to the stream," she whispered. "Nick will be looking for us there."

Jeff's expression was resolute, yet when she moved to get up, he gestured her back down.

"Wait," he said. "Let me."

"But..."

Jeff was already pulling himself out of the little shelter. Armed with his birch club, he slipped back onto the path. He took two steps to the left and listened, ear cocked back the way they'd come. Then he turned and took a few steps in the other direction before stopping to listen. Heather listened, too, but there was nothing except the sound of a few birds and the chuckling stream in the distance.

Jeff nodded, satisfied, and hefted the club up on to his shoulder.

"Looks like we're good," he said and started to turn back towards Heather. "You can come out now-"

He froze and all the color drained from his face.

Heather, already climbing back to her feet, turned. The forest was moving, lurching, lunging towards Jeff. But even as she watched, the green and oranges faded and turned, coalescing into a familiar gray figure with a damaged shoulder.

The Mechanic's roar shook the air. Heather jumped, lost her footing and fell on her back. The alien never even glanced at her. It was too busy charging at Jeff, who stood swinging his club, looking for all the world like a little boy, facing off against a monster.

Which wasn't that far from the truth.

Jeff swung. The alien reached.

Heather's heart caught in her throat. Her hands felt about the ground for ammunition.

"JEFF!"

Heather's shout did what she wanted it to do: it made the alien jump and turn towards her. Her hand found stone and she hefted it.

Aim for the shoulder, hit the shoulder, Nick's already wounded it there...

But then Jeff did what he shouldn't have done. He shouted too and, worse, ran ahead, swinging the stick. The alien whipped back around and swatted at him. This time, the human was too nimble. Jeff dancing out of reach, swung again, shouted, and then began to run away. The alien gave chase and as it ran, it reached for the weapons in its belt.

No, no, no!!

Jeff and the Mechanic disappeared around the corner.

Heather grabbed another rock and scrambled to her feet. She began to run, only to catch her foot on something unseen. She fell hard, skinning her hands and ripping a hole in her jeans. She heard Jeff shout again, this time in pain, and her heart squeezed in kind. Then through the air, the ripping whine of sawing wood ripped through the air.

The lasers!

She gained her feet and ran.

Rounding the corner, she found them. Abandoning the path, Jeff was now running in a zig-zag pattern down the steep side of the mountain, heading towards the edge of the jagged outcropping that overlooked the stream. He had lost his club, but still shouted like a crazy man to keep the monster coming. From Heather's vantage point above them, she could see that despite the tight trees, the alien was clearly gaining and Jeff was about to hit the edge.

Jeff, Jeff, what are you doing?

Then alien stopped running. It positioned itself carefully, and stood with the weapon in its hand, tracing Jeff's movements.

It's a gun!

Before the thought could fully register, the weapon spoke.

Jeff yelped and wood cracked. He was beside a giant old oak and as Heather watched, chips flew. A huge bough, heavy with orange and red leaves, fell. Jeff saw it and threw his hands up, but he was too close to get away. He disappeared under the falling mass of wood and leaves.

Heather's heart stopped.

Jeff! She wanted to scream, but no sound came out.

The alien began to move forward cautiously. Heather moved, too, recklessly leaping from rise to rise, heedless of the noise she was making. Like her, the Mechanic was too focused on the pile of leaves and wood to notice.

Don't move, Jeff, oh, please, don't move!

He'd said that the aliens could only see movement, but this one didn't seem to have much of a problem locating him. It stopped short a few feet away, gun at the ready, and chirruped loudly. Then it looked around.

Heather, now maybe a hundred yards away, froze. The Mechanic's gaze slid right over her, chilling her to the marrow. Then, apparently satisfied, it bent over Jeff and chirruped again.

It's trying to get him to move. Oh, stay still, Jeff, stay still.

Heather worked her way closer, circling around the alien so that she was now coming up on its right. She didn't really know what she could do. She couldn't confront the alien, not without some sort of weapon. But if Jeff was hurt…

The alien bent over again and reached out. Heather stopped, breathless, panic coursing through her. She could see more of Jeff now. One foot was free of the leaves and an arm lay within inches of the alien's wide, clawed foot. But neither moved and she couldn't see his head or detect any breathing.

The alien reached out and tentatively touched the bough. When that didn't move, it reached shook it, chirruping so piercingly that Heather threw her hands up to her ears. Jeff didn't stir a muscle.

The alien took a step back and Heather dropped behind a screen of bushes. The alien chirruped again, hefting its weapon up defensively. It scanned its surroundings, its eyes sliding right over Heather's hiding spot. Then it took a step back from Jeff.

Heather's heart rose.

It was leaving! It was leaving and maybe Jeff…

But then the alien pulled one foot backwards as though to kick. Heather rose to do something, anything, to stop it, but it didn't kick. Instead, it placed its foot on Jeff's prone body and pushed. And before Heather could do anything at all, it had shoved Jeff and the heavy tree limb over the side of the outcropping.

A scream rose to Heather's lips, but for once, she managed to swallow it. She dropped back down among the bushes, pushing her fist into her mouth, biting on her hand until she tasted blood, trying with all her might to keep silent and still.

The alien went to the edge and looked over, its large eyes unblinking even in the sharp afternoon sun. Then, with a motion of its head that was almost like a nod, it holstered its weapon and went striding back up the hill, leaving Heather alone.

CHAPTER 13

Nick raced through a dense clump of young birches, squeezing between tree trunks and taking branches full in the face. His heavy backpack pulled on his back and caught on branches. More than once it crossed his mind to shed it, but there was no time even for that. Full-on panic had him firmly in its grip and he was too terrified to stop.

That coyote never had a chance...

Behind him, the thrashing sounds of the Hunter's approach slowed for a moment, as though it, too, needed to catch its breath.

Stay still for just a moment...

The birches gave way and Nick stumbled out into a clearing. Enormous oaks spread their thick branches overhead, grandfatherly and noble, not that Nick had much thought for their appearance. He was too busy trying to catch his breath and figure out what to do. Behind him, the thrashing had ceased, but it was too suddenly still for him to believe that the creature had left. It was somewhere in the woods and had stopped for some reason.

Nick raced behind the first big oak and stopped, pressing his back against it to catch his breath.

Think! Think, Nick!

He began to race through the list of things he knew.

They are fast. They are strong. They can change color. They are determined to kill us. They have weapons.

So much for the negative side. On the other hand, Jeff's theory about their vision seemed to hold true.

They can't see without movement.

A breeze sent the leaves into a sighing chorus and from across the clearing, the thrashing began. Long, slow, steady footsteps drew near.

Nick didn't have any time left to think. He grabbed the first low branch and began to climb. The bark bit into his hands. His sides, aching from the run, screamed anew, but he ignored this. He ignored everything but his newly established goal – to conceal himself among the dancing red and gold leaves.

The thrashing grew louder and the footsteps drew nearer. Nick pulled himself up one final branch and froze when the birches exploded and the Hunter stumbled into view.

Nick had managed to climb about twenty feet from the ground, getting among the remainder of the ageing leaves. Even from his high perch, the creature was enormous. Its oblong grey-green head swung back and forth as it stepped further into the clearing. It held the laser gun at the ready, its long powerful arms tense. It moved carefully, like a man hunting a small, annoying rodent. It did not fear Nick. It had no reason to fear him.

The Hunter paused under Nick's tree. It looked around in all directions except one. It did not look up.

Don't look up, don't look up, don't... Nick gripped the tree tighter.

The Hunter stood perfectly still for what seemed like ages. The only movement that Nick could detect was the jaw, jutting in and out like it was chewing. The eyes, too, liquid black and unblinking, glinted with movement. It was catching its breath, probably. Perhaps it smelled Nick but couldn't locate him. Maybe it thought that Nick had its sight limitations, too, and hoped that by waiting, Nick would move.

Just don't look up...

Sound slammed into Nick like a wall, nearly causing him to lose his grip. The alien was screaming.

The sound ripped through the air, long and eerie, a flushing technique that very nearly worked. Nick's hands slipped, his foot knocked against the tree with a clunk and only the very volume of the alien's cry covered the sound. He recovered, though only barely, and clung to the tree, pressing his face against the rough bark, praying as he'd seldom had cause to pray, that the alien would not look up.

Mercifully, it did not. The Hunter swung its head back and forth, listening, watching. When it called again, Nick was prepared. A moment of silence passed. Then, apparently satisfied, the alien moved off, stepping out from under the branches of Nick's tree and disappearing into the trees beyond.

Nick waited a long time in that old oak, clinging to the trunk, listening as it groaned in movement. The leaves danced in the breeze, and the sound of birds returned to the clearing, but still he waited, listening, watching, feeling his heart return to normal. He fully expected the creature to return at any moment. But the clearing below remained empty and no sound could be heard over the normal sounds of mountain life.

He was alone, yet he clung to the tree like a frightened child.

Instinct cautioned him against moving. Every fiber in him screamed that to move was to expose himself. But Heather and Jeff were out there somewhere, alone and without a weapon. He had to find them. He had to get them home safely and warn the others. He'd promised his father. More than that, he'd promised himself. He had to go.

Still, Nick hesitated. The aliens had proven once before that they were capable of hiding and, worse, of changing their skin color to blend in. Nick's vision was obstructed by the very trees that were shielding him. How could he know that the alien was really gone?

The pistol was in his waistband, the backpack heavier still on his back. Nick rested on a thick branch and leaned his torso against the trunk of the tree. Getting the backpack off was difficult. Sweat had soaked through his shirt, gluing the straps to his shoulders. When he finally managed to rip it off, he nearly lost it through tired hands. But he held the backpack fast in his left hand while pulling out the pistol with his right.

Four shots fired. Four left.

His aim would have to be good.

He held the backpack over the ground, his heart pounding, the pistol grip slick in his palm. He waited a second for his heart to steady – then he released the backpack.

It fell hard, hitting branches as it went down and sounding as loud as a body breaking through the tree limbs. It hit the ground with a heavy thud, dust and pine needles curling up around it.

Nick clutched the tree trunk and his pistol and waited.

Nothing happened.

The backpack's fall had made a suitable sound and fury, yet nothing emerged from the trees to challenge it. This meant either the alien's eyes were sharper than he'd thought, or no one else was around to see it. From what he'd observed of the alien, he'd have to assume the latter. But there was only one way to be sure.

Nick tucked the pistol back into his waist, released his grip on the branch, and forced himself to climb down slowly, one branch at a time.

He fully expected to be attacked the moment he jumped down from the last branch. But though he braced himself and landed on legs like rubbery noodles, nothing reached for him. No laser-blade ignited, no cry echoed through the empty woods. He was, for all appearances, alone on the side of Stark Mountain.

He hesitated a few moments, scanning the trees, looking for any sign of… anything. But he could distinguish nothing from the wood and, worse, knew that he would probably not be able to see anything even if it was there.

You can stand there staring until you starve to death or you can damn all and move.

Heather was out there, alone, with only Jeff for protection. He had to find them, find them and bring them home.

The sun was dropping low in the sky and the air was taking on its nightly chill. Soon it would be dark. Twilight fell quickly in the mountains, where overhead coverage of trees blocked the light even at the height of noon. The backpack lay at his feet, heavy with food stuffs and a medical kit. They'd probably have need of both before the night was through.

I hope I remembered to pack the flashlight.

He probably hadn't. After all, they weren't meant to *be* on the mountain overnight...

It was supposed *to be just a simple hike. Who knew we'd run into... And they're still out there, somewhere, maybe just over that...*

Nicholas Miller didn't finish the thought. He didn't know where the aliens were and with their ability to camouflage, he could walk by them at any moment and not know until it was too late. He didn't know where his sister was or how long they had until the invasion began. What he did know was that he had to find the one and report the other and neither could be done if he didn't start moving.

He grabbed the backpack, slipped the straps over his shoulders and began to walk.

CHAPTER 14

Heather raced to the side of the incline. Below her, the ground broke away sharply, creating a nearly sheer drop where nothing could live and little could grow beyond the occasional foolhardy young pine or maple. At the bottom of this drop, a stream chewed through dark earth and smooth rock. Heather had found the stream that Nick pointed out to them earlier, but she barely noticed it. Her eyes were caught and held by the sight of the scorched oak branch, suspended midway down the hill by several groaning young trees.

Jeff!

She threw herself into the descent, half climbing, half falling on the loose earth and slippery needles that coated the hillside. Even as she clambered downward, the tree shuddered and shifted, the weight of the heavy beam almost too much for the slender trees that held it. If Jeff woke, if he shifted, he could bring the whole thing down on his head.

If Jeff's still alive...

She squashed that thought along with the one that wondered about Nick. There would be time enough to panic later. Well, probably there'd be time to panic...

Her feet slipped on the soft dirt. Heather couldn't stop herself from sliding into the tree limb. It shifted on impact, pulling away from the side of the mountain, and she clutched at it. It was a useless gesture – if the limb had decided to fall or one of the trees it rested against gave way, its weight would have pulled her from her precarious perch and dragged her down the hill after it. But luck stayed with her. The limb moved out, then back and rested. It would hold, for the moment.

She breathed a sigh of relief and let go, taking a moment to catch her breath and steady herself.

"Jeff?"

The name came out unsteady and soft, hardly more than a hoarse whisper. It was certainly no competition against the sound of running water and she raised her voice and steadied it for the second call.

"Jeff? Where are you?"

There was no answer and no blue jacket among the tattered leaves and branches. Heather rose to her feet, unsteady against the sharp incline, and grabbed hold of a thin branch to steady herself as she looked around.

"Jeff! Je-"

A groan cut her off mid-sentence. She craned her neck and just barely caught a glimpse of a battered blue sleeve.

Jeff!

She scrambled around the tree limb and slid down the hillside until she came to a halt beside him. Jeff lay where he had fallen, face down, his head half covered by leaves and his own arm. Branches and leaves covered his leg. He wasn't moving.

Heather worked her way around towards his head. She reached out to shake him, and then hesitated as half-remembered injunctions against touching a wounded person resurfaced. More daunting was the idea that he wasn't...

No. No!

Then her eye caught the slight rise and fall of his back and relief flooded her. He was alive at least.

She touched his shoulder, at first gently, then more firmly, shaking him.

"Jeff? Jeff, wake up!"

He stirred, groaning and she automatically hushed him. He stretched and raised his head. His face was scratched and blood, clotted with twigs and dirt, covered his cheek. But he was alive and his eyes, though confused, were clear.

"Heather?" he whispered as he started to prop himself up. "What hap- oh!"

His face contorted with pain and he dropped back down. "Oh, man, that hurts."

"Where? Where does it hurt, Jeff?"

"Might be easier if you ask me where it doesn't hurt," he retorted then his head shot up. "The alien…!"

"It's gone for now. We've got to get out of here. Can you move?"

"Sure," he muttered. "Sure, I can move, I can do this, sitting up is easy, easiest thing in the world, a child could do it, a toddler, an infant even…"

He shifted and rolled himself upright. He looked even worse sitting up. He was coated in mud and pale from pain. Blood from his face wound had soaked his collar and heightened the pallor of his complexion. He touched his head, wincing.

"Dizzy," he whispered.

"Can you walk?"

"Yeah, yeah…" He propped his feet underneath him and made as though to stand, only to gasp aloud before dropping back down on the ground.

"What is it?" she asked.

"My leg," he muttered through gritted teeth. "The ankle… it's… it's bad."

It must have been. Sweat beaded his brow and the strain made his face rigid. She put a hand on his shoulder and was about to tell him not to worry, to take his time, when the relative quiet of the waning afternoon was broken by a sound. It was like the alien's chirrup, but different. If Heather had been forced to describe it, she would have probably said it was something akin to a siren or a warning claxon. It chilled her right down to her toes. And it *definitely* wasn't human.

Shoot. Oh shoot...!

Jeff was looking up now, his pain forgotten in the sudden reality.

"Was that...?" he asked and Heather nodded.

"We've got to find someplace to hide," she said. "Come on, I'll help..."

As she said this, another sound caught her attention: it was fresh wood, snapping.

Her head jerked upwards. The tree limb was moving, shifting against the steadily weakening trees - and they were right in its path.

As she watched, the restraining trees gave way and the bough fell.

"Jeff, move!"

She shoved him out of the way and rolled herself. The tree bough rolled, gathering speed as gravity caught hold. It fell and hit the ground where they'd just been with a shattering impact that sprayed Heather with twigs and acorns. The disintegrating remains of the tree bough rolled all the way to the stream and sent up a cascade of water.

Heather and Jeff lay where they were for a minute, catching their breaths and listening to the sound of the trees and the birds. Then Jeff turned to her.

"Imagine that," he said. "We've outrun aliens with lasers and then nearly got killed by a tree branch. How stupid would *that* have looked on our obituaries?"

Heather didn't know what to say to that. Overhead, an answer chirrup reminded them of their real problems.

She scrambled to her feet.

"Come on," she said. "Let's put some distance between us and them. Lean on me."

Jeff might have been thin, but his lanky form weighed heavily on Heather's shoulders. The slippery hillside made their descent even more difficult and there were a few times when

Heather thought they were going to fall. They walked without speaking, reserving their strength for the descent and their attention for more intruders. Heather knew that Jeff was in pain from the way he breathed – heavily when he took a wrong step, shallow when he strained. But he didn't complain and he didn't speak.

Somehow, they managed to make it to the bottom without losing their balance. Obeying Nick's instructions, they turned and went upstream. The air here was fresh and cold, smelling of moss and wet earth. Supporting Jeff here was complicated by the extremely narrow bank that lined the stream. Heather put her right foot into the stream several times, the shock of the extreme cold causing her to gasp and stumble. Overhead, the sun was starting to drop below the tree line. They didn't have much daylight left.

Jeff stumbled again and Heather knew she'd have to give both of them a break soon. There was a curve in the stream and when they rounded it, she found a small gap in the hillside. Too small and shallow to be considered a proper cave, it was nevertheless large enough to conceal them both from any prying eyes overhead. She turned their steps toward it and Jeff's sigh of relief was audible as she lowered him down.

"Oh boy," he said. His glasses, now scratched and stained with mud, were crooked on his white face. He looked awful, and sharp intakes of breath testified to the pain of his ankle. Yet still he did not complain. He pulled himself backward into the cave with his hands and shifted to the left so there was space.

Heather helped him, and then stood.

"I'll go and see…" she said and he interrupted.

"You can't go back out there!" he objected. "They might be anywhere!"

"I know," she said. "But Nick's out there, too."

His face darkened. "Oh. Right. Okay."

He began to move as though to come along, but she stopped him with a hand on his shoulder. "You stay here. I'm just going to take a quick look, then I'll be back."

"But, Heather, I really should…"

She didn't let him protest. Instead, she pulled off her jacket and threw it at him.

"There's a first aid kit in there," she said. "And some trail mix. I'll be back to look at that ankle. Stay put, okay?"

She left before he could protest.

Their cave had been created in the hillside by the roots of an old tree spread out like a canopy over a patch of ground that must have been eroded by the stream's changing levels. From markings in the embankment and the hillside, Heather could see where the water had risen, probably in response to melting snow on the mountains in the spring time. But rising and falling water levels couldn't hold her interest now. She grabbed hold of a small tree, growing bravely in the steep ground, and hauled herself up.

It was easier climbing up than it had been going down. This was likely because she was not as frightened as she had been – Heather was still scared, but the feeling had receded until it was merely a background noise, like the chill of her wet foot or the hunger pangs that were beginning to gnaw at her stomach.

She gained the top of the hillside and crouched low at the edge. The path continued on here, narrower and more tightly hemmed in by the trees on one side and the drop on the other, where Heather was. It was darker now, for the sun was falling behind the pines.

She waited a few minutes, but nothing stirred beyond the occasional branch in the breeze or the chatter of squirrels, winding their way up and down the trees.

They wouldn't be playing if there were aliens around, she thought and then amended, *But can they see them? Would they know what the aliens are?*

It was impossible to say, of course. She would have to take the risk. She hauled herself up and onto the trail.

Instantly, she looked around. Again, nothing moved, nothing breathed, nothing chirruped. By all her senses, she was alone.

Hurry up...

Heather ran up the path one way, back toward the landing site, listening and looking, her heart pounding in her chest. She halted when she reached a bend and had to stop herself from calling out Nick's name. After all, he wasn't the only one out there to hear. Instead, she listened, steadying herself, slowing her breathing, listening for some tell-tale sound beyond the usual noises of the woods. But there was nothing and the path was growing dark.

He's not here. Not yet.

He would come, if he were able, of that Heather had no doubt. Nick knew that she would follow his instructions. This path was probably the quickest way back to the truck. If he assumed that they were moving, he might decide to stick to the path rather than climb the steep slope to the stream below. He would have no idea that Jeff was hurt and they were stopped. He was observant, but not psychic.

Young trees grew alongside the path. Heather grasped one of the thin branches and twisted it until her hands were sticky with sap and the branch, broken, drooped, pointing down to the path. Then she reached into her pocket and pulled out a small black scrunchie. She wrapped it around the limb.

Find it, Nick...

She raced back down the path until she reached the spot where she'd come up. There was no point in running ahead – if Nick passed the path beyond where their new-found cave was, Heather wanted him to keep going. The sooner one of them got help, the better.

Though if he doesn't come, I'll have to get Jeff out of here all by myself.

It was a daunting prospect. The terrain was rugged, they were literally on the run from alien beings that wanted to kill them, and Jeff, who was taller, heavier, and clumsier than she, was quite possibly incapacitated with a bum ankle.

One problem at a time, Heather, one problem at a time.

The ground was churned up where she had come up and young trees grew here too. She did the same as before, making sure that branch pointed, not over the path, but down the slope. She pulled the pink wrap elastic out of her hair and wrapped it around the end, then hopped down the hill.

She nearly lost her balance, but caught herself and turned back to smooth the sides of the trail, making it less obvious that someone had been there. Someone like Nick wouldn't be fooled, but the aliens, unused to everything about this planet, might just be.

Unless they can track by scent... Oh, man, Heather, why did you think of that?

She panicked, then got hold of herself and reasoned. If the aliens could track by scent, they'd shown no evidence of it. Anyway, there was nothing she could do about it if they could. Best just to keep moving.

Her work done, Heather paused a moment and looked up and around, brushing the hair out of her eyes with a dirty hand. It was quiet, too quiet. She longed to hear Nick's big boots crunching through the woods, but she heard nothing.

Be safe, Nick.

The woods whispered back to her, darkness closing in like a cloak. Heather stood in the gathering gloom, listening for footsteps.

"The world's a ticking time bomb," Jeff had said earlier and for the first time in Heather's life, she knew beyond all reasonable doubt that he and the others had been right. The world was on the brink of disaster. And the human race had run out of time to prepare.

This can't *be it. Oh, Lord, this can't be it!*

No time for this, Heather! Get back to the dugout.

With that, she turned and went back down the slope to where Jeff was lying, waiting for her.

CHAPTER 15

J eff hadn't moved except to take inventory of the supplies in her jacket. He was tense, sitting bolt upright, but he relaxed when he saw Heather. His bad ankle lay propped in front of him on the remains of a small rotten stump.

"I'm glad you're back," he said, adjusting his scratched glasses. The lenses glinted dully in the fading light. "Everything all right?"

"Yeah, no signs of anyone," she said.

She didn't want to say, *Including Nick,* for fear the words would stick in her throat. She didn't have to say it out loud – the look on Jeff's face showed that he understood. They were alone in a world on the brink of destruction, and Heather's heart could barely handle the pressure.

Stay focused, she thought. *Whatever you do, now is* NOT *the time to cry.*

Jeff was watching her carefully and his gaze felt like a gentle interrogation, one she could not afford to submit to. She took a deep breath and gestured towards his ankle. "You didn't take your sneaker off."

"I was afraid if I took it off, I wouldn't be able to get it back on," he said and winced as he adjusted his sitting position.

"Good thinking." Heather hunkered down and began to carefully peel back the pant leg. She stopped when Jeff tensed up. "Am I hurting you?"

He appeared bashful.

"It's an awful mess," he said and blushed.

It hadn't occurred to Heather that he might be embarrassed for her to see him like this. The thought was oddly flattering.

"It's all right," she said soothingly. "I've been through first aid training with my aunt, who's a nurse, and again through the Girl Scouts. I've seen a lot of sprained ankles. Besides," she turned back to his ankle and began to coax the mud-encrusted denim up his calf, "we've got to get you mobile."

He braced himself. "Yes, you're right about that. We can't stay here."

No. No, we can't...

Because Jeff was wearing sneakers, she could see almost the entire ankle without removing the shoe. The sprain was a bad one. Already it was swelling, mottled purples and angry red mixing in declaration of the wound. She untied the shoe and loosened the laces.

"How is it?" he asked.

"Pretty bad," she admitted. "We have to stabilize your ankle. It's a pity you're not wearing boots." She thought a minute then got up. "Stay here and keep it elevated. I'll be right back."

Outside of the cave, away from Jeff's presence, she breathed a little easier. The forest was as still as ever. She scanned the ground for branches until she found a fairly strong, thin, fresh branch with smooth bark. She pulled the leaves and smaller twigs off and smoothed it in her hand. The stream gurgled and suddenly she was thirsty. The water tasted of earth and snow and was cold enough to make her gasp. She thought about bathing Jeff's foot in it, but though the cold would help, she couldn't risk not being able to put the shoe back on him. The truck was too far away to make it barefoot.

When she returned to the dugout, she found Jeff scribbling madly in a notebook while holding her penlight in his mouth. He looked up when she came in.

"Found something to brace your ankle," she said, holding up the sticks. "Do you have a handkerchief?"

He nodded and pulled one out of his back pocket. It was neatly folded and the top edge was stained with dirt and tree bark, evidence of his fall and their recent adventures. It was just large enough for the job. She laid it on his knee and turned to the stick. With an effort, she broke it over her knee. It was a new branch, still moist with life, and it didn't break cleanly. She had to twist the two pieces until her hands were coated in sap and the final stubborn wood fibers gave way.

"What are you doing?" Jeff asked. He had forgotten he was holding the penlight in his mouth and it fell into his lap as he spoke.

"Bracing your ankle," she said. "I'm going to loosen your sneaker and stick these on either side of your foot, and then tie them at the top with the kerchief. It'll be uncomfortable, but it should make it easier for you to walk." She took a rock and began to rub it over the bark of the branches, making it smoother. "What are you working on?"

He glanced down at his notes. "My observations about the creatures. It might be helpful when we talk to the authorities."

When. Not *if.*

She swallowed back her fear.

"Good thinking," she said, forcing herself to speak calmly. "I think you might be right about their vision, so we should move in the dark."

He nodded, his eyes growing dark with doubt. "Yeah... About that..."

"What?"

"Well, I was thinking, since they can't seem to see well in the daylight, they probably rely on their other senses more heavily, like their sense of smell or their ability to hear, for instance."

Her movements slowed. "You mean, like bats?"

"Could be."

"Which means at night…"

His face was impassive. "It could give them an advantage at night."

That was an unpleasant thought. Suddenly the sounds of nature around them grew very loud, like a thick wall preventing them from detecting the predators outside the perimeter. It took Heather a second to shake the chill.

"I'm not waiting here all night," she said firmly, determined to keep the panic from her voice. "We have to get back to warn the others. We have to – we can't afford to wait and I've seen what they can do in the daylight."

"You're right, of course," he said. "It was only a theory. Anyway, it is imperative that we alert the authorities before these creatures can complete their mission, whatever that mission is. We have a duty as citizens and as earthlings. I was thinking, that since I've been wounded and you are still mobile and nimble, our best chances of getting the word out there in a timely fashion would be for you to go on by your…"

She stopped him midsentence by slapping him on the thigh with her stick. "If you offer to nobly stay behind, I'm going to hit you over the head with this."

"It's not about being noble, it's about doing the right thing, the best thing, the…."

"I'm *not* leaving you behind."

"But…"

"Jeff, if you don't go, I don't go. We'll both stay here and either freeze to death or be eaten. I'm not going on alone. There are only two options and that's it. Got it?"

He hesitated before nodding. "Got it."

"Good."

They were silent for a moment. Heather wondered if she should start applying the brace. But Jeff looked comfortable and they still had an hour or two before total darkness, so she decided against it. She put the sticks aside and looked for someplace more comfortable to rest, rubbing her arms to ward off a sudden chill.

"We'll both stay here and either freeze to death or be eaten..."

The careless remark came back to her, along with images, stark and grotesque. Memories of Jeff's crumpled body under the tree limb and Nick running off into the woods with the monster on his heels competed with imaginary scenarios of getting caught, of the claws ripping into their bodies, of blinding fear and overwhelming pain and icy death....

"It's the scout ship, obviously."

"Heather, we've been invaded!"

Oh, Nick!!

Heather buried her face in her hands.

The whine of the laser ripped through her imaginings, followed by the crackle of burning wood. She felt again the weight of the alien as it had stood over her and the smell of sulphur that followed in its wake. Incongruously, she thought of her family gathered at the campsite, enjoying their reunion, laughing, eating, talking, minor rivalries lost in the overall warmth of kith and kin. They were oblivious to the threat. Oblivious and helpless.

Nuclear war had been frightening enough. This... this was far, far worse.

Margot's taunting question rang in her head: *"Where will you be when the apocalypse comes?"*

It's begun. The apocalypse is here, it's now!

"Heather?"

Jeff sounded concerned and close, but she could barely hear him over the sounds of her own sudden sobs.

"Such a small ship. For an invasion, I mean."

"Space: the final frontier. It's where we'll have to go, after World War Three."

Only they couldn't go there. Not now. Not when that was where *they* had come from.

"Heather?"

We're trapped here, on this planet, sitting ducks, easy targets. Oh, God, I was wrong, I was so wrong.

She shoved her hands into her mouth to stifle the sound and desperately tried to rein in her emotions. But she was helpless against the tide of terror and sorrow that washed over her. Her shoulders heaved with the effort and tears poured through her fingers.

We are lost. We are all lost...

An arm snaked around her shoulders. Somehow Jeff had managed to put himself beside her. Heather leaned into him, one hand grasping the fabric of his coat, her tears soaking his shirt. She could hear the beating of his heart and it was both soothing and a torturous reminder of what was at risk.

I'll lose you. I'll lose everyone...

His hand made circles on her back.

"It's all right," Jeff said, in a muffled tone. "Nick'll be fine. We'll find him, Heather. I promise, we'll find him and then we'll get home and everything will be all right."

Empty promises and baseless reassurance.

"Then you think war is inevitable, too. War and annihilation."

"War is, definitely. You don't just stockpile nuclear arms for fun, you know."

She'd argued for years that the Russians were only human, that as long as they could talk and find some common ground, war could be avoided. It was all academic now. The invaders weren't human and there was no common ground.

She gripped his coat even more tightly and gasped through a sore throat, "You were all right, Jeff. You were all right. It is inevitable."

His hand slowed. "What is?"

It was hard to speak. "War."

We won't get the chance to destroy ourselves — they are coming to do it for us...

Jeff didn't even try to argue. His arms just tightened their hold.

Heather's sobs came harder, pulling up from her gut, almost to the point of pain. She managed to keep it quiet, though, crying into his coat until she was wrung out and exhausted. Jeff, for once, said nothing. He simply held her, a silent, comforting presence on a lonely, suddenly hostile planet.

CHAPTER 16

Heather's breakdown was intense, but short-lived. It left her feeling shaky and cold and it was only with effort that she pulled herself out of Jeff's comforting embrace.

When she did, she insisted on going out to get Jeff something to drink. He declared he was fine, but she wouldn't listen. She emptied the plastic baggie of trail mix onto his notebook, took the penlight with her and, turning her face away so he couldn't see the damage done by her tears, left in search of water and a few minutes of privacy.

Foolish pride, she thought, but she wasn't able to override it.

She hiked up the hill and checked the trail again, but if Nick had come by, he'd left no sign. The woods were dark, the trees black whispering sentinels, but the sky was turning pink and gray. It was late, but not late enough to risk heading back.

Heather carefully scurried back down and washed her face in the stream before filling the baggie with water. She stood then, stretching her back out and listening. There were no chirrups, no sounds of wood cutting, no engine sounds, nothing out of the ordinary. The lack of sound was worse than anything she'd heard all day.

She brought the water back to Jeff and found him bent over, poking his ankle.

"How does it feel?" she asked.

"All right," he said. "It doesn't hurt unless I touch it."

"You still have feeling, right?"

"Sure – why?"

That was good –there was little she could have done if he'd gone numb. She didn't answer the question, instead handing him the baggie of water. She already known he'd lied about his thirst, but seeing the way he gulped down the water bore testimony to the extent of the lie.

"It's still light out," she said. "We've got an hour at least before it's fully dark."

He nodded, swallowing. "Good."

She was aware that he was watching her, anxious, no doubt, that she might fall apart again. So was she, truth be told, but she kept her anxieties firmly in check. She had to.

She dropped down in the dirt next to him. "Got any of that trail mix left?"

"Of course. I wouldn't start without you."

They resettled against the back of the dugout. The trail mix was her mother's own salty blend of peanuts, cashews, raisins, and chocolate chips. The protein was hearty and the chocolate a welcome taste of home that nearly got Heather crying again. She choked back her emotions, glad the dugout was too dark for Jeff to see.

They munched in silence for a little while, relaxing in spite of everything. Heather was surprised at how natural it felt to sit with Jeff's shoulder pressed against hers, his hand brushing her own as he passed her the mix. It felt oddly right, as though the previous tensions were eons and centuries away from where they were now.

Amazing how aliens can bring people together, she thought and immediately regretted it. The very thought of the predators outside sent a shiver running down her frame. *Best not to think of anything... Be like the Karate Kid. Breathe in, breathe out, breathe in, breathe out...*

She'd almost achieved a sort of empty-headed peace when Jeff broke through the quiet: "Feeling better?" he asked.

The memory of her earlier outburst brought a hot flush to her face.

"Yes," she said, quickly. "I'm fine."

"Right," he said. "It's okay, you know. I mean, it's only natural."

"You mean because I'm a girl?" she asked, with a bitterness that surprised even her.

Jeff was certainly taken aback by it.

"No, of course not," he said. "It's only natural that you should be frightened. I'm frightened, too." He threw another peanut into his mouth.

"You're frightened? But you predicted this!" she snapped, though she could hardly have said why she was angry. "You and Nick, you both said that war was inevitable."

He turned away from her, picking at the trail mix.

"It's easy to talk about these things before they happen," he said. "It's quite another thing when they actually happen. But you were right, too, you know. It was never inevitable. We humans could have worked things out. As long as we can understand one another and talk, we can always work things out. Now... Well, it's hard enough to understand humans, let alone..."

"Alien creatures from another planet?" she finished.

He nodded and she could feel his fear through the chill air.

"Yeah," he said. "I didn't expect this."

"Who could have? Amoebas are one thing. This... This is like a bad movie at the drive in." That last line reminded her of Nick and she sighed heavily. "God, I hope Nick is okay. I wish... Oh!"

Tears were trickling down her cheeks again. She pressed her hands into her face. "I'm sorry. I'm sorry, I just... It's the not knowing, you know?"

Jeff's sigh was weighty. "Yeah," he said softly. "I know."

They sat in silence for another long moment. Heather felt, again, the weight of probable annihilation resting on their shoulders and longed to break the silence before it broke her. But it was Jeff who managed to speak first.

"I know what it's like for you, worrying about Nick," he said. "I felt the same way when my mom disappeared."

She craned her head to look at him, but his face was shrouded in shadow. "Your *mom* disappeared?"

"Yeah. When I was a kid, back in Florida." He looked down at his hand, toying with a few pieces of the trail mix. "One day I came home from school and she wasn't there. I was, maybe, seven or eight. It was… it was rough. Not knowing where she was or if she was alright. My dad was frantic, as you can imagine. He sent me to live with my grandmother while he looked for her. Took him three weeks."

Heather was stunned. In all her ruminations about Jeff's past, something this dramatic had never occurred to her.

"What had happened?" she asked, almost afraid of the answer.

He shrugged. "She'd run away. Her sister, my aunt, was hiding her out in her house in Miami."

Heather was glad that the darkness was obscuring her expression. It was obvious from the way Jeff spoke that he'd reconciled himself to his mother's actions, but the betrayal was more than Heather could swallow with calm acceptance. Mothers simply didn't run away from their children. That was a breach of an unspoken contract, a violation of trust, a betrayal of a magnitude beyond Heather's imaginings. She thought of her mother, her grandmother, her aunts and older cousins. For all their various imperfections, this was one mistake she couldn't imagine them making. Husbands and wives split, but mothers couldn't divorce their children. It was unnatural and Heather couldn't imagine how that must have made young Jeff feel.

After a moment, she asked, "Why?"

Jeff shrugged again. "Who knows?"

He was lying and they both knew it. Heather waited, picking at her trail mix, letting the lie dig deeper and deeper into Jeff's conscious until he finally shifted in his seat and admitted, "That's not strictly true."

"No?"

"No." Jeff's voice sounded odd now, as though he were speaking through some obstacle. "She told my dad that she'd never really wanted to be married. That she... didn't really want to be a mother. She had felt pressured or something, I don't know. Anyway, my dad tried to persuade her to come home, but... well, she wouldn't come back." He shrugged for a third time. "That was that."

"Did you ever see her again?"

"She used to come on my birthday. Lately, she... Well, I'm not a kid anymore, so..." He shook his head and examined the remains of the trail mix on his notebook with real interest. "Anyway, I just wanted you to know, I understand. It isn't easy when you don't know where someone you love is."

"Jeff, that's just... awful," Heather managed.

"It's harder on my dad," Jeff said. "It isn't easy, you know, raising a kid on your own, with no family around to support you. He does all right, but it isn't easy." He moved the trail mix around with his finger. "He doesn't complain. He told me that the only thing he regrets is that he only has one son. He was an only child too, you see, and he wanted a big family. Now it's just him and me. It's good, you know, but still."

"Yeah," Heather said. "I know."

But she didn't, not really. She had Nick and her parents and grandparents and so many aunts, uncles, and cousins that holidays were chaotic, birthdays frantic, and family reunions enormous and noisy affairs. She didn't know what it was like to be lonely. She'd never had a chance to find out.

Heather thought of the first time she'd seen Jeff in school, remembered the bright - though guarded - light in his eyes, his general awkwardness, both social and physical. She pictured her mother and thought of how hard she leaned on her. She wondered what her life would be like if she didn't have confidence in the support of her family. She decided that she never wanted to find out.

She recalled her conversations with Margot and how nervous Heather had been to admit that she liked the awkward new kid, even as a friend. She wondered if Jeff had noticed her reticence.

Of course he must have. How could he have missed it? And the thought hurt her deeply.

It is stupid to let Margot dictate who I hang out with, she thought. *No more. I'll be a friend to whomever I please.*

His arm was resting against hers in the cave and, in a brave moment, she threaded her arm through his. When he turned to her, startled, she smiled through the darkness.

"Guess you'll have to hang out with my family more," she said. "I have more than enough to spare."

She couldn't see his face in the darkness, but she felt his body relax. He turned toward her and in the dim light of the penlight, she saw his face ease into a smile.

"That would nice," he said softly.

For the second time that day, she wondered if he was going to kiss her. His face was close, his breath brushing her face, and her heart quickened in anticipation.

Then something snapped in the wilderness outside.

Someone or something was approaching.

Heather jumped and managed not to squeak, though only just barely. Jeff's grip tightened on her arm and he drew his legs in and looked around, but there was no weapon except the sticks that Heather had brought to brace his ankle.

There's no defense! We can't move! This was a stupid, stupid *place to hide!*

Heather reached down, snatched the sticks up, and pulled back, handing him one. It would do no good – if the aliens knew where they were, they only had to use the lasers – but having a weapon restored her faith in herself somewhat.

Whatever happened, she might be able to land one blow before...

Outside, the footsteps moved closer and closer. In a moment, they would be able to see feet, or paws, or whatever you would call the alien limbs.

Crunch. Crunch. Crunch...

Closer, closer....

And then sturdy brown boots clumped in view and a peeved voice cut through their fear.

"Good grief, Heather," Nick complained, bending until they could see his pale and dirty face in the dim light of the dying day. He held out the pink scrunchie. "Can you two be any louder?"

"Nick!"

Heather was never so relieved to be interrupted in all of her life.

CHAPTER 17

Nick was tired, bruised, hungry, and annoyed to discover his sister cuddling with the beanpole Jeff in the middle of the woods. He was too relieved to complain about any of these things. The kids were alive. Banged up, especially Jeff, whose ankle looked about the size of a baseball, but alive.

Heather and Jeff weren't so frightened that they hadn't made a few good choices. Heather's treatment of his ankle was as well-done as possible in the circumstances and although Nick wasn't too keen on waiting around, he had to admit that Heather was right – they stood a better chance moving in the dark.

They made room for him in the dugout and sat in a half circle, a strange reminder to Nick of the times he and Heather used to play camping in the woods behind their home. He handed around the bottle of water that mercifully survived the fall from the tree and told them of his adventures while the other two ravenously put away the granola bars he'd brought in his backpack. They were starving and with good reason – it had been hours since breakfast and terror has a way of chewing through calories. Nick wished he'd brought more to eat, but how was he to know they'd wind up stranded in the woods, waiting for nightfall? Earlier in the day, when this was just a slightly annoying outing, he hadn't thought to pack more than what would see them through a lunch and a few snacks. Tonight was the annual Miller family barbeque and Nick had been looking forward to his father's special Texas-style hamburgers.

Now, watching the others eat and picking through the stale trail mix Heather had given him, the very thought of his father's specialty was enough to set his stomach growling and his heart thudding.

Even if we get back, we won't have time to...

Whoa, what's with the 'if'? It's gotta be 'when', man. You won't make it otherwise.

He spoke out loud to keep morbid thoughts away. "You were right about those things being half-blind," he admitted to Jeff, tossing the remains of Heather's trail mix into his mouth. "They only see with movement."

"During the day, that we can tell," Jeff corrected.

Heather piped in with, "Jeff thinks they may have night vision, like bats."

Nick's mouth went dry.

Why would you say that, you idiot? Like Heather need to be worried about that, too, on top of everything else.

Wouldn't do to say *that* out loud, not with Heather watching him.

"Well," he said, glaring his disapproval at Jeff. "Let's hope you're wrong about that."

The two kids exchanged looks and Nick knew, with an older sibling's sudden flash of insight, that they were holding something back.

"What gives?" he demanded, looking from one to the other. "Come on. We can't be in any worse position than we already are. What is it?"

Heather turned pale. Nick braced himself for bad news... And he took the loss of Jeff's camera very badly.

"I can't believe it." He grabbed at his hair and pulled, a childish habit he only reverted to in extreme stress, like learning they'd lost all the evidence to prove Earth had been invaded. "I just can't believe it. We took all that risk, almost got killed, and you had to go and drop the only evidence we have that aliens exist. Great work, Spock, great work."

"It wasn't Jeff's fault," Heather said, which sounded ridiculous, because it was totally Jeff's fault. "We were all scared and running."

"We are in this mess because he decided to take the pictures in the first place!" Nick retorted. "Now we have *nothing* to show NASA. We almost died for nothing."

"The pictures are still on the camera," Jeff said. "I know exactly where I dropped it. All we have to do is go get them."

Nick nearly choked.

"Go *get* them?" he sputtered. "Go back and *get* the camera?"

Jeff exchanged a worried glance with Heather. "Yes," he said slowly. "As in, retrieve the camera. The fall may have damaged the camera, but the film is probably okay."

Heather nodded. "It takes a lot to destroy it. All we have to do is slip back and…"

"NO!" It was all Nick could do to keep from roaring. He moderated his tone, but not his fury. "We are *not* going back there! We barely got out alive the first time and now *he's* injured. We'll be lucky to make it to the truck!"

"Well we can't leave without it," Jeff said. "No one will believe us."

"I don't give a…" Nick stopped himself from swearing and instead leaned forward. "Look, Peg-Leg Pete, if you think I'm going to risk my sister's life going back to fix a mistake *you* made, you're crazy."

Jeff was surprisingly unmoved. "If we go home without the camera, we will not be believed until it's too late."

"I don't care."

"Earth is being *invaded*, Nick! If Earth is going to mount any kind of defense, timing is of the essence and we may already be too late!"

Nick was not about to be lectured on responsibility. "My first responsibility is her safety and yours. We're going home."

"You can't just decide that!" Heather protested. "Everything is at stake and we need that film, Nick — we haven't a shot unless we can prove what we saw."

This whole conversation would have been ludicrous if it didn't happen to be true. As much as Nick wanted to argue with his sister and her boyfriend, as much as he wanted to pull rank and force them to bend to his will, as much as he wanted to go home and hear his father say, "We've got this, Nick," he knew, oh, dammit, he knew they were right.

Timing was crucial. And their human weaknesses had already eaten up far too much of it.

They were right, but not entirely. Heather had only barely gotten away alive last time. He wasn't about to risk her or Jeff again.

So he threw up his hands in frustration and gave them a partial victory. "Fine, fine! You're right."

"We are?" Jeff blinked in surprise. "Great, then we can..."

"Hold it, Space Boy. You aren't going back. I am. Alone."

"But *you* don't know where it is," Jeff said. "I have to go."

"We don't have three days for you to make the journey," Nick snapped.

"Well, what do you suggest?"

"I'm not suggesting. I'm ordering. You two go back to the truck. I go back and get the camera."

"That's insane!"

"He's right," Heather said. "You can't go alone, Nick. It's too dangerous."

"My responsibility..."

"*Our* responsibility," she snapped. "It's not just about us, Nick. It's about everyone. Literally *everyone*."

"Heather, I am *not* going back to tell Dad that I lost you to an alien crew because of some stupid camera."

"You won't have to," She folded her arms. "Either we all make it home or none of us do."

Nick's fury was beyond the boiling point.

"Then forget it," he spat. "We go home without the camera, end of story."

"But we can't!" Heather cried out and Jeff nodded.

"Heather is right, Nick," he said. "We can't let you go alone and we also can't go home without the camera. I know where it is. I can get it more quickly than you can."

"And if we all get killed, what then?" Nick demanded.

Heather's face went a shade whiter, but Jeff merely leaned forward, his glasses glinting in the darkness.

"That option has occurred to me," he said in a calm, steady tone. "That would be unfortunate, but, on the bright side, if the worst were to happen, our disappearance would be almost as convincing as the camera."

That got Heather's attention as well. The two siblings stared at the bespectacled outsider.

"That's the *bright* side?" Nick demanded. "The *bright side*?! If the worst should happen, Levinson, we'll all be dead!"

"We have no idea what the aliens' intentions actually are," Jeff began and at that, both Millers started talking.

"They almost *killed* you, Jeff!" Heather protested as Nick growled, "I spent an hour of my life trying to outrun gray-green goons with guns, hell-bent on silencing me. I rank myself as an expert on their intentions."

Despite the double assault, Jeff was implacable.

"Let's say the worst happens, right?" He leaned forward, his glasses glinting. "We're killed or taken captive – it doesn't make a difference which. If we don't come home, our families will worry and the authorities will be forced to search for us. In searching for us, they will find traces of the landing and the laser damage."

"Things they will still find when they go to investigate our story."

"*If* they decide to investigate our story. It's October. The parks are shut down for the season and most of the staff have been let go. The state has no interest in paying overtime, not when winter rescue missions are coming up. Now imagine three teenagers, who were lost in the woods, come home spouting stories about alien invaders. How quick do you really think they are going to be to follow up on *that* lead? Wouldn't they far rather write it off to loser kids dealing drugs and suffering from delusions?"

Nick stared at him. Was Jeff really saying what he *thought* he was saying...?

Heather asked the question for him.

"So, we'd be better off disappearing altogether than going home without the film?"

Jeff barely hesitated before nodding.

"They'll be forced to look into *that*," he said. "But if we go home... well, there would be next to no pressure to check out our eye witness testimony. No one will believe us. Not without evidence. Disappearing obviously isn't the best option – it'll take the authorities far longer to discover the truth that way, but it's still better than just going home."

"*Dying,*" Nick clarified, "is better than going home."

Jeff looked at him, his face white but his eyes steady.

"In this scenario," he said, "yes."

"The good of the many," Heather said.

Jeff turned to her. Their eyes locked on to each other. "The good of the many," he whispered.

Oh, for the love of...!

Nick cursed under his breath and ran a hand through his hair. He wanted to shake the pair of them, but they were right. Without that camera, they were just three crazy kids who'd possibly smoked something they shouldn't have. No one would believe them. Even with the film, they'd be dismissed initially as loonies – pictures could be forged after all. But when scrutinized, the veracity of the picture and the stories would hold up. A picture was worth a thousand words and he wasn't about to gamble on the aliens' good intentions.

Besides, there was every indication that, insist as he might, Jeff and Heather would go on their own anyway. He didn't know Jeff at all, but Nick knew his sister and when her jaw was set the way it was now, he couldn't talk her out of anything. And there was no way Nick was going to let them do this on their own.

Nick didn't like this at all. But he'd been backed into a corner.

"All right," he said reluctantly. "We wait until dark. Then we get that camera and get the hell out of here, right?"

The other two nodded solemnly. Nick had the sudden impression that he was signing all of their death certificates... but there was nothing else to be done.

"So we wait," Heather said.

"We wait," Nick nodded, then added, "Lucky for us, there's a moon out tonight. We'll be able to see better."

She nodded, then looked at him. "Won't they as well?"

He ignored that.

"'Into the valley of death rode the six hundred,'" Jeff muttered softly, his voice resonant with feeling. He gained in volume as he fell deeper into reverie: "'Tis a far, far better thing...'"

"Shut *up*, Spock!" Nick growled and experienced a fleeting moment of pleasure in the shocked silence that followed.

CHAPTER 18

Time crawled. The dugout was cramped and cold and the ground they were sitting on was gravelly and moist. Nick's legs, warmed by his extensive work out that morning, soon grew stiff. Pain, kept at bay initially by adrenaline, began to seep into forgotten cuts and bruises. The low ceiling prevented him from stretching to his full length, but these were all minor grievances compared to the anxiety that weighed on him like a jacket made of bricks.

They were in hostile territory, alone and cut off from civilization. They had no more food and their only weapon of real worth was the gun tucked into his waistband. Nick's best plan was to lead his sister and her crippled boyfriend *back* to the alien encampment in the hopes of finding the camera with the evidence to convince the authorities that an invasion was eminent. Jeff's best second best case scenario was that they die doing so.

It was the kind of story Hollywood made cheap movies about, but there was nothing remotely charming about living it in real life. Still, Nick wasn't so terrified that he couldn't see the bright side. Providing they survived the encounter, this was going to be one sick story to tell his dorm-mates.

If they survived the night, that is. And if Nick went back to college. Which, of course, he couldn't, not now.

The planet is going to war. There is no longer any such thing as business as usual…

It was too great a realization to absorb, not when he had to keep his mind and body ready for the task ahead. Despite what Heather and Jeff thought, Nick's primary responsibility was his sister's safety. The trick was finding a way to ensure it.

One step at a time, one problem at a time. That's what Dad always says. You don't have to know the whole answer to the problem, just figure out the first step towards solving it.

He calmed his mind and thought through what they were going to do, mapping out the best and quickest routes towards the landing site, calling to mind the tree coverage along the way. No more wide-open trails for them, not until they were a good distance away from the not-so-little green men and were sure they weren't being followed.

Nick shifted and felt the pistol digging into his hip, a reassuring discomfort. He knew, from the one shot that he landed, that the aliens weren't impervious to lead, which was good news. The bad news was, he only had four bullets left - that is, if he'd counted correctly. Looking back on the events of the past few hours, he couldn't be entirely sure how many times he had fired.

Checking the weapon would only aggravate the others' nerves, so he waited. When Heather and Jeff, sitting side-by-side at the far end of the dugout, began a whispered conversation, Nick slid the magazine out and pulled the bullets out one by one. Three. And there was one in the chamber. He turned the barrel so that it faced outside and racked the slide.

There was no disguising that sound. Both Jeff and Heather jumped and Heather squeaked, "What is it?" in a high pitched, terrified voice.

So much for the brave girl who was going back by herself, Nick thought sardonically. Aloud, he said, "Nothing to worry about. Just checking the ammo." He loaded the rounds back into the magazine.

"How many?" Jeff asked.

"Four," Nick said and slapped the magazine back into the grip. He racked a round into the chamber, then set the safety on. "And there's three aliens."

"So we can afford to miss once?" Jeff uttered a helpless little laugh.

Nick gave him a look that could have withered a pine tree on the spot and everyone subsided into silence.

Jeff began to write again, holding the penlight with his mouth. The scratching sounds of pencil on page sounded loud in the quiet. Heather craned her neck to look at what he was writing. After a moment, Jeff handed the book and pencil to her. She read, grinned, and began writing herself.

Kids, Nick thought. All the same, he was glad they'd found a way to occupy themselves while waiting. If only he could find some way to do the same.

An hour passed, then another. Nick dozed off and on, waking at the slightest of sounds from the outside world. Nothing out of the ordinary happened. Heather nodded off, too, resting her cheek on Jeff's shoulder, her face relaxed and peaceful in the dim light.

Of all of them, Jeff alone seemed to keep alert. He kept writing long after he and Heather had finished their written conversation, bent over his book, frowning in concentration. The squeak of lead on paper was almost hypnotic. Nick wondered what on earth was so fascinating that it must be written at this time. He didn't ask. He didn't feel like being subjected to one of Jeff's long-winded explanations.

Jeff caught him watching and gestured to the page.

"A report," he said. "For the authorities."

Nick nodded, wondering if anyone was ever going to read it. He was surprised when Jeff, instead of chattering on, turned back to his work.

Nick waited until nine o'clock, roughly an hour and a half after sunset. He checked his watch, and then rolled over and out of the dugout without a word to the others.

The air outside was clear and cold and refreshing after so long stuck in the cramped interior. He stretched, feeling his back pop in relief. His legs were stiff and he shook them out as his eyes adjusted to the darkness. As predicted, there was a moon: almost full and bright through the tree coverage when clouds didn't scuttle by to cover it. What Nick could see of the sky was promising: the clouds were moving fast and the light and darkness alternated with them. He and the others could take advantage of the shifting pattern and perhaps not be forced to use the few flashlights they brought with them. Hopefully Jeff was wrong about the aliens being able to see better at night.

They could just as easily be day creatures, who sleep at night like humans, Nick mused. *Let's hope anyway.*

Nick craned his neck to study the star patterns, wishing, as he often did, that he'd spent more time studying astrological charts. Reaching into his backpack, he pulled out a battered black compass, gift from his Boy Scout group a few years ago. The glow-in-the-dark needle spun under scarred glass, settling on the north quickly. Nick may not have been familiar with the stars, but he knew the mountains and the local terrain as assuredly as if he'd grown up on the side of Mount Stark. He could find his way both to the landing site and to the truck he'd parked on the road without a problem. It was the hostiles they might encounter along the way that worried him.

That and one other thing: he'd surprised Heather by going to Mount Stark this morning instead of the easy climb she'd expected. What Heather didn't know was that climbing Mount Stark had been a last-minute decision, one he'd made while on the road. Which meant no one back home knew where they actually were, a stupid decision under normal circumstances and only worse under these. If the worst did happen, Jeff was right to think that search parties would go out, but they would go to the wrong mountain first. It could take days before they found Nick's truck – and who knew how long before they found the landing site.

The kids didn't know this, though Heather might guess, given enough time. Nick wasn't about to enlighten them. His focus was on getting them back to the truck in one piece.

I promised Dad I'd keep everyone safe. I'll keep that promise if it kills me.

Funny how often one could say that in the course of a lifetime, never realizing that one day, the words might be more than just hyperbole.

He ducked back down into the cave and found that Heather was already awake and working on Jeff's ankle.

"We'll be ready in a minute," she said. Her hands worked with the sticks and kerchief nimbly, making a sturdy brace for the weakened limb. Aunt Linda, the nurse, would have been proud of the work.

Nick kept his voice low. "We go through the woods and keep to the shadows," he said and was gratified when the others leaned in to listen. "There's a moon out, so we use the flashlights only under extreme necessity. And no talking."

"Naturally," Jeff said and gave a snappy salute. "We maintain radio silence at all…"

"Jeff."

"Right!" He mimed zipping his mouth shut and subsided.

Heather just nodded.

"We'll move as quickly as we can," Nick said. "No unnecessary risks. We have an obligation to get back home to tell people, *even* though it would more convincing if we all died at the site. No *harakiri* noble nonsense, not on my watch."

He glared at Jeff, expecting lip. But Jeff merely nodded, looking bright and eager.

Heather finished tying off the ankle and sat back. "How does that feel, Jeff?"

Jeff blinked and lifted his leg. "Well, um…"

Nick cut him off. "You can't tell until you try to walk on it. Come on, let's go outside."

He exited first, looking and listening for any invaders before helping Heather pull Jeff out of the cave. Once Jeff was out, he waved away their helping hands and took a few wobbling steps.

"It's fine," he said. "I can move."

Heather looked uncertainly at Nick, but Nick ignored her. It was their idea to go back for the camera, not his, and they had known better than he about Jeff's physical state. They'd made up their minds – they weren't going to change them now.

He pulled on the backpack and tucked the pistol into his waistband. "You lost the camera where, exactly?" he asked.

It was difficult to make out facial expressions in the dark, but he could clearly see Jeff's embarrassment as he shifted uncomfortably.

"Behind the embankment," he said. "Where we were first surprised by the aliens."

Of course you did, Nick wanted to say.

"All right, let's go," he said. "Follow me and *be quiet.*"

Heather nodded resolutely and took hold of Jeff's arm. Jeff looked surprised by the gesture, but seconded the motion by putting his hand on hers.

Nick took a deep breath, swallowed his fear and his resolutions and turned. It was time to go and all he could think of was that verse from the old Psalm, *"Lo, though I walk through the valley of the shadow of death..."*

Part Three:
THE SHOWDOWN

CHAPTER 19

Heather had always been afraid of the woods at night. The trees, comforting sentinels in the warmth of the daylight sun, became sinister when darkness fell. They seemed to absorb the darkness, to hold it as a wall obscuring unknown numbers of dangers from her sight, threats that could be anything from ghosts to wolves to men. As a child, she'd gotten into the habit of pulling the curtain in her bedroom window to secure the light and warmth of her bedroom from any encroachment. As she grew, she learned that most of her shadowy fears had been just that – shadows. But the base fear never left her and every night, she pulled that curtain between her safe room and the dark and dangerous outside world.

Tonight, however, there was no curtain, no comforting room filled with light and noise to hide in. She was out in the darkness she'd always feared, following Nick and Jeff up steep hillsides and into brush and the thick shadows under the pines. There was no sound except for the breeze that rustled the branches overhead and the noise of their own footsteps, crunching through the underbrush. Despite Nick's warnings, there was no way to avoid making noise.

Chills ran down her back, a cold that had nothing to do with the cool night air. She focused her attention on matters at hand, on trying to avoid snapping twigs and breaking the branches that they brushed past. She watched Jeff like a hawk, noting every stumble and every wobbling step he took. The brace helped, but judging from the spasms that contorted his frame from time to time, he was concealing a great deal of pain.

He shouldn't be walking on that ankle, not until it's properly treated, she thought. But there were things more important than personal health. Reasons that had them heading, not to the safety of Heather's cozy room and the curtains that kept out the world, but back towards the landing site where hostiles waited.

This is the stuff nightmares are made of. And yet here we are.

She trudged along behind, having a vague idea of their direction and the distance between them and the alien ship, but her knowledge was based on her familiarity with the trails. Nick didn't stick to the trail for very long and Heather was lost shortly after they left them. Sickening dread pooled in the pit of her stomach even as Nick kept walking with confidence, as though he knew exactly where he was and where he was going. She could only hope that appearances matched reality.

Hang in there, Jeff. Hang in there…

They'd been hiking through the darkened morass for what seemed like forever when Nick called a halt.

"Catch your breath," he whispered and sat on a stump, studying his compass.

Jeff leaned against a pine, breathing heavily, his eyes squeezed shut. Heather pulled out her penlight and flicked it on, scanning the ground. She'd just found what she was looking for – a long, stout branch – when Nick's hissing caught her attention.

"Put that *out!*" he whispered.

She did immediately, and stuck her tongue out at him in the dark. She found the branch, broke off the small twigs that grew off of it, and brought it to Jeff. She felt for his hand and pressed the branch into it. She could sense his confusion and stood on tip-toe to whisper into his ear, "Use this as a crutch."

He squeezed her hand gratefully.

"Let's move," Nick said.

And they were off again, moving as quietly as they could through the woods, trying not to stumble when fallen branches snaked up around their legs like snares or living limbs struck at their faces. The moon overhead was a beacon, blinking as the clouds moved past, both friend and foe as the illumination helped Nick find his way while exposing their movements. But nothing emerged from the shadows around them. Nothing charged or chirruped and no laser lit the gloomy atmosphere. It was all as still as a mountainside ever was – and yet through the stillness one could detect the beating heart of life.

Heather had just gotten into her stride when Nick called a halt again, this time silently. They were behind a cluster of short bushes, wild blueberries if Heather were to make a guess. Up ahead, a hilly incline loomed up through gloom of night. Nick crouched behind the blueberry bushes and gestured for Jeff and Heather to join him. When they were gathered so close that their shoulders touched, Nick gestured to the clearing beyond.

"We're here," he said.

Cold fear washed over Heather again and through the shocked silence, she made out a sound that before now had been lost in the general hum of a living forest: it was the sound of a small engine.

"Is that the ship?" she whispered.

Jeff shook his head. "Sounds too small..." he mused.

"Quiet!" Nick interrupted then turned to Jeff. "The camera – where did you drop it?"

Jeff bit his lip and thought. The clouds shifted over the moon, plunging them into temporary blindness. His words came through the dark. "It was where I first fell. The strap was loose and it broke when I got up."

"Where you first fell," Nick repeated. "Right."

The clouds shifted again and a weak light fell over his face. Heather could see Nick studying the terrain, judging the distance and squinting to see through the gloom.

"I could find it in a…" Jeff started to rise, but Nick grabbed his arm and held him.

"Forget it," Nick said. "You're staying right here."

"But…"

"I said forget it. You'll be too slow."

Heather's heart began to thud in her chest, slowly but hard. They were really going to do this. Nick was going to go out there and…

The consequences of failure, a distant thought when this mission was a theory in the dugout, hit her forcefully now. She reached out to grasp Nick's sleeve, her mouth opening to tell him not to go. But the words didn't come and Nick's sleeve slipped out of her grip. He grabbed her wrist and cold steel touched her hand.

"Take this," he was whispering as Heather's finger curved automatically around the pistol grip. He pulled her closer until his mouth was practically on her ear. "You stay here and if anything happens to me, you *leave*. You go home and take Jeff with you. Promise me."

"Nick…"

"Promise!"

His voice sounded hoarse and desperate. Her eyes stung, but she managed to mutter in a numbed voice, "I promise."

"Give me the penlight."

She pulled it out of her pocket and handed it to him. He took it, let go of her arm and wrapped her in a quick, hard hug that ended abruptly. Then he shrugged off the backpack and handed that to Jeff.

"Anything happens," Nick whispered, his voice like a dagger in the night, "you get her home."

Jeff opened his mouth, then shut it again and nodded.

"You can count on me," he whispered.

There was a beat. And then Nick said: "Yeah… I know, man. I can."

Heather whispered, "For goodness sake, quite talking like it's the end, Nick! You're coming back. Just hurry up."

Nick nodded. He waited until clouds slid over the moon again, then, with a deep breath, he pushed through the bushes and out into the clearing.

He disappeared out there in the darkness. Heather and Jeff rose as one to watch, but the darkness was complete and he might as well have jumped into a black pit. Only when the penlight came on, with a tiny snap that sounded like a gunshot in the tension, did they finally catch a glimpse of him. Even then, they could only really see the light, bouncing like a marble over the grassy, pine-needle-choked ground. This way and that, it played in tight, careful circles, moving further and further away from the safety of their hiding place.

Come back, Nick, come back…

Heather couldn't even whisper the command. She looked around, but it was impossible to tell if there was anything watching out there. All was black as pitch and noisy as the leaves on the trees. She couldn't even hear the sound of Nick's footsteps anymore. The only way to tell that he was even out there was the light of the tiny penlight…

And then the light stopped. It hovered for a moment over one spot, then dropped and they could faintly see the outline of Nick's knee. There was a hesitation and then the light went out.

"Nick…"

Jeff's hand gripped her shoulder, killing the unbidden whisper.

The breeze shifted and the tree grew loud again. Clouds scurried across the sky and the clearing was suddenly drenched in moonlight. Nick's dark figure knelt in sharp relief against the newly lit field. He had the camera in his hand. He raised it triumphantly even as he got to his feet. He'd found it – but he wasn't the only one moving on that field.

The chirrup sounded at the same time as the blast of static. Something white and light streaked across the open ground. It struck Nick in the chest, knocking him off his feet and sending him several yards backwards before collapsing into a broken pile.

From the opposite end of the field, where the beam had come from, a gigantic shadow detached itself from the shade of the trees. It was the Hunter.

The pistol fell from Heather's numbed hands. She forgot everything but Nick's prostrate body and the enormous creature that was lumbering for him. Without thinking, she flung herself at the rise, trying to climb up, over the bushes, to get to Nick before the Hunter did. Something was stopping her, pulling on her jacket. Jeff's arm snaked around her waist and his hand covered her mouth. She tried to kick herself free, but both of them fell backwards on to the root-rutted ground.

She fought viciously, but Jeff was stronger than he looked. He held her tight, whispering urgently, "It's too late, Heather, it's too late!"

She closed her eyes and forced the scream back down her throat. Tears coursed over her cheeks, wetting Jeff's hands. The nightmare had come true and there was no waking up from it.

CHAPTER 20

Nick! Oh, Nick!

Breathe, Heather, breathe. Keep it together, keep it together. You've got to get Jeff home and... oh, Nick!

Heather lay with her back on Jeff's chest, her eyes blinded with tears, her mouth covered by Jeff's hand, and her heart shattered in a million pieces. The only thing keeping her together was the steady beat of Jeff's heart, just slightly off-set from her own, and the rise and fall of their breathing.

Breathe... Breathe... Breathe...

This wasn't supposed to happen. Brothers didn't die like that. They died in car accidents or overseas in foreign fields or in hospitals of old age. They weren't struck down by monsters in the middle of the night on a mountain...

Breathe... Breathe... Breathe...

She tried closing her eyes, but all she could see was his body, flying backwards to crumble on the ground like a mannequin. He hadn't even had time to shout out...

She gasped in pain and opened her eyes again.

Breathe, breathe, breathe...

Jeff was shifting under her. He wanted to get up. Probably couldn't breathe with the weight of her body on his chest. He tentatively loosened his grip on her mouth, but he needn't have worried. She was beyond sound now.

"I'm going to look, Heather," he whispered.

She let him push her off. She curled into a fetal position, breathing, breathing, breathing, not letting herself do anything but breathe.

Oh, Nick, what am I going to say to Mom and Dad?

"If anything happens to me, you leave, you got that?"

It's like he knew... When he pressed the gun into my hand, he knew...

The gun...

There was a snapping sound. Jeff must have knelt on a twig, for she heard the sharp intake of his breath as he braced himself for an onslaught. She braced herself, too, but the monsters must not have heard. In a minute, Jeff's noisy breathing resumed and she relaxed.

That short moment of panic was enough to clear her head. She couldn't stay there. Neither could Jeff. Nick had left instructions and this incident wasn't just about them. If she and Jeff didn't warn everyone, camera or no camera, it wouldn't just be Nick's body left crumpled in the dust. She had other people to protect. So did Jeff. They had to move.

She sat up, wiped the tears from her eyes, and began to look for the pistol. She pushed herself onto her knees and felt about in the dark. Her fingers touched cool metal just as Jeff's hand tapped her shoulder.

She looked up. Jeff was gesturing towards the clearing. He wanted her to look.

Heather's stomach dropped. The last thing she wanted was to see Nick's body again. She'd break down. She'd lose her nerve and they'd be lost...

But Jeff kept gesturing insistently.

She got up and peered over the hedge, just in time to see the dark outline of a gigantic shape, the monster, the Hunter, before it disappeared over the ridge in the direction of the space ship. It was just light enough to see that the alien was carrying something, thrown over its shoulder like a sack of potatoes.

Heather's eyes went to the spot where Nick had fallen. It was empty.

"It took him!" she whispered in horrified disbelief. "It took Nick!" She flashed-back to the first time she'd seen the Hunter and the blank face of the deer that had hung suspended from its shoulders, and rage mixed in with horror.

"It was examining him," Jeff said. "Maybe he's still...!"

"They're going to eat him," she said blankly and lifted the pistol. "I won't let them."

Jeff's hand clamped down on her gun hand, pinning her in place.

"No, Heather, wait..."

"Let me go..."

"Heather, listen. I don't think they took him to eat him. I think they're keeping him prisoner."

She stopped wriggling and stared. "A prisoner... then that means..."

Jeff nodded. "There's a *chance* Nick is still alive."

Hope flared up, almost as painful as grief. Heather looked into Jeff's eyes.

"A chance," she breathed. "I've *got* to know for sure."

He was already nodding.

"Me too," he said. "Let's go."

***

The hum of the ship's engines grew louder as they climbed the short ridge up to the top of the overlook. The very air seemed to vibrate with tension. Heather couldn't keep from scanning the area as they moved. After all, Nick had been taken by surprise. She and Jeff could just as easily be taken.

Despite his injury, Jeff moved almost as quickly as she did, although he did slip clumsily twice on the ascent. She caught his arm the second time and hauled him up with her. Both dropped to their knees when they got to the top and paused, listening.

But nothing fired up to kill them and no monsters emerged from the darkness.

As they knelt there, panting, it occurred to Heather that only a few hours had passed since they'd last seen this hill. Only that afternoon, Nick and Jeff had been arguing about the likelihood of amoebas existing on another planet, and all of them had been blissfully ignorant of the truth. In those few short hours, their world and their understanding of the universe had completely changed forever.

"Look!"

Jeff's whisper sounded like a shout in the tension-filled silence.

Heather started. Jeff was already crawling to a newly made gap in the brush blocking their view to the alien spacecraft. It was, she realized, the spot where the alien had carried Nick through. She crept over to join him.

Little had changed at the crash site. The ship lay where the alien had lifted it, as solid as ever. Lights had been brought out and carefully positioned to shine on the ship without lighting up much of the sky. A few bundles and canisters lay in organized heaps around the site. One pile was covered in a tarp. The engines hummed steadily, with only little fitful bursts to indicate that there might be a problem.

Where's the...?

Even as she thought of the question, the Mechanic appeared from around the other side, its giant head swinging back and forth as it moved. Its shoulder bore a new patch and as they watched, it exercised the arm, moving it in slow circles.

That's where Nick hit it, Heather thought. Her grip tightened on the pistol grip.

The Sentry was trailing behind the Mechanic. She could barely hear its faint chirrups as the pair rounded the nose of the ship. The Sentry chatted as the Mechanic lifted its hand, pointing it towards the ship. And then there was no ship.

Heather's heart skipped a beat. The Sentry squealed in triumph but even as it cheered, the engines coughed and the ship reappeared. The Mechanic made an annoyed gesture.

"It was invisible," Jeff whispered. "That's why we didn't see it fall. It was shielded somehow."

That thought made everything worse.

The two aliens shrugged off the apparent failure and moved towards the piles of supplies. The Sentry was chatty, the Mechanic decidedly less so. It stopped by the tarp and stood staring at it, moving the sore arm in slow circles, ignoring the Sentry, its mind obviously elsewhere.

"They don't look worried," Heather whispered.

"Would you be if you were them?"

The ship shimmered and the Hunter appeared, stepping out of the ship with ease and grace. It was alone and empty-handed.

"Where's Nick?" she whispered.

Jeff didn't reply. The Mechanic and the Hunter began a discussion, limbs moving in time with their black jaws. The Sentry capered about in easy circles around them, one ear on their discussion, eyes out on the woods beyond. It didn't contribute to the conversation, which Heather was having a hard time determining whether it was a heated discussion or an outright argument.

Then, with a dramatic gesture, the Hunter bent down and pulled the tarp away. A pile of barrels obstructed most of their view, but Heather could see enough to recognize one thing: a denim-clad leg with a familiar boot.

Nick. They are arguing about Nick!

She craned her neck, studying the leg, trying to make out movement.

Come on, Nick, give me something!

But it was too great a distance and she couldn't see that far.

The Sentry moved further and further out from the two quarrelling aliens. Whatever their issue was, he kept his focus on security, though his pattern was irregular. He was smaller, too, which made him an unlikely guard, but Heather didn't have time to concern herself with how the aliens assigned tasks. She leaned forward further and it was Jeff that had to pull her out of the Sentry's line of sight.

The Sentry paused and stared. He must have spotted their movement, but he didn't signal the others. After a moment, he resumed his wandering. His two companions kept on arguing and Jeff and Heather relaxed.

"What do you think?" Jeff asked. His eyes, framed by the now-battered wire-rim glasses, looked huge in the moonlight.

Heather shook her head. "I can't tell if he's alive or…" She couldn't finish the sentence. Instead, she took a breath and said, "I can't leave him here."

Jeff was silent for a moment. She could guess what he was thinking. He was probably thinking they should obey Nick and get back home before they were caught too. That they didn't know if Nick was alive or dead; that they were risking their own lives and the lives of others by staying here. And he was probably thinking a rescue was impossible.

He'd be right about… well, all of that. They were risking their lives when they had a duty and an obligation to go home and warn the others. But none of that mattered to Heather. She sat in the dark, holding Nick's pistol, and knowing she could not leave until she was sure he was dead. If Jeff decided to go home alone, she wouldn't stop him.

In fact, she really ought to encourage him to do just that. She could give him time to get away, then slip closer to the camp, close enough to see whether her brother was breathing. If he was, she'd get him out. If he wasn't, she'd leave. The likely outcome in both cases was capture and death, but she honestly didn't see any other way around it. It had to be done. Family came first.

Jeff would argue. He'd tell her she was being stupid, that Nick wouldn't want her to risk her life, that she owed to her parents and so on and so forth, but eventually he'd give in and go. He wouldn't want to die here. He wouldn't want to leave his father alone, and someone had to get back to warn the planet.

Jeff stirred, breaking her thoughts. Heather braced herself. He'd argue and she'd let him go on until his argument wound down and he was tired. Then he would leave and she would stay behind and that would be it.

If only she didn't have a lump in her throat the size of an eagle's egg.

When Jeff opened his mouth, she was prepared for the barrage, but not for what he actually said.

Jeff said, "I agree. Let's figure out a plan to get him out of there."

Heather almost fell down. Then she almost knocked him over when she hugged him.

***

"Listen to those engines," Jeff said a few minutes later.

The two larger aliens had concluded their discussion and the Mechanic had headed around to the other side of the ship. The Hunter had taken an armful of supplies into the ship while the Sentry loitered on the outskirts of the circle of light. As she surveyed the scene, Heather found something vaguely familiar about it, something that touched on an old memory. She couldn't quite put her finger on what it was.

Nick's body, now a little more visible, was still and silent.

"We can wait until the Sentry goes to the other side of the ship," Heather suggested. "That one seems to go back and forth."

Jeff nodded. "But we don't know if the alien inside the ship can see outside."

He was right. By the looks of it, the ship was one solid mass of steel, but since the aliens could move freely through the sides of the ship, the two humans really had no clue as to its composition.

Jeff was chewing on his fingernails, his eyes glued to the landing site, oblivious to the dirt that coated his hands and fingers.

"What we need is a distraction," he said. "Lure them away from the ship so we can slip in and check on Nick."

"Right," Heather agreed. "What do you suggest?"

Jeff glanced at the heavy pistol, tucked into her waistband. She placed a hand protectively on the grip.

"We can't waste the bullets," she whispered.

He nodded slowly, his eyes dark with concern. He was worried about the same thing she was. Even if they managed to distract the aliens long enough for one of them to get to Nick, how were they supposed to get him out of there? Jeff was injured, and she wasn't strong enough to haul Nick on her shoulders. Even if she could, they couldn't out run the animals and she didn't know where to hide.

Nick would know what to do...

"Maybe we should wait until he wakes," she suggested.

Even as she spoke, the engines roared to life. Heather jumped, startled, and they both turned to see the Mechanic rounding the nose of the ship, chirruping in triumphant. The Hunter emerged and clasped hand-claw-paw with the Mechanic. Excitement fairly radiated off their bodies. The ship, it appeared, was repaired.

"Shoot," Jeff muttered.

The engines coughed and stuttered. The aliens released one another. The Mechanic made a motion, a motion that Heather would have judged to be 'don't worry' and moved to the other side of the ship. The Hunter watched it go, then looked around the clearing, scanning the woods.

Heather had to stop herself from dropping behind the bushes – even the slightest movement could betray their presence. She could feel, rather than see, Jeff's body tensing beside her.

Apparently they weren't seen. The Hunter grabbed another armload of stuff, chirruping loudly before it disappeared into the ship again. The Mechanic was behind the ship. The Sentry was nowhere to be seen.

Heather relaxed enough to whisper, "We're too late!"

"Wait." Jeff's arm clamped down on hers. "Look!"

He was pointing towards Nick's prone body. She stared – and saw nothing but his leg.

"What is it?" she asked.

"You missed it. He twitched."

"He *twitched!*" Her heart skipped a beat.

"Nick's alive," Jeff said. "And I'm guessing they aren't going to leave him behind. Hand me the backpack."

"*...aren't going to leave him behind...*"

Of course they wouldn't. Why leave behind a perfectly good human specimen, one that could be studied and prodded and dissected...

Heather stopped herself from thinking. She wordlessly handed the backpack to Jeff and he ripped it open, for once careless of the sounds he was making. The engine's roar covered them anyway. Heather kept her eyes on the landing site while Jeff studied the contents of the backpack.

The Hunter emerged from the ship, arms empty. It went and stood over Nick for a second, studying him. It raised its foot and Heather half-rose in response, but all it did was nudge Nick gently. Nick didn't move. The Hunter hesitated for a second, then grabbed another armload and trudged back into the ship.

Neither the Sentry nor the Mechanic were visible.

"We've got to do something, Jeff, and quick," Heather said. "They suspect Nick's coming around."

Jeff nodded and threw the backpack onto his shoulders.

"I was hoping there was a flare or something," he said. "Okay, here's what we do." He pointed to the tree line a little distance away. "I'm going to head out in that direction and draw their attention by throwing things. When the aliens come to check it out, you slip in and get Nick. Follow that line of bushes and keep out of sight as long as you can. If I shout for you to drop, do it and keep still. They won't be able to see you in this light. Keep the pistol with you, use it if you have to. Got it?"

Heather looked down at the landing site, noting the cover provided by the bushes. If she could get Nick into the shadows, they could remain still and hide. It was an incredibly dangerous plan, but they had no other option.

She turned to see Jeff blinking at her.

"I'll keep them away from you as long as I can," he said.

"They'll catch you."

His chin rose. "They won't. Anyway, I don't see any other way."

Heather didn't either.

"But what you said earlier," she whispered. "About it being better if none of us... I mean..."

She couldn't finish the sentence, but Jeff nodded and shuffled his feet uncomfortably.

"Right," he said, finally. "Well, I- I mean – You aren't... I couldn't..." He stopped, then met her eyes and grinned sheepishly. "I guess... Some arguments are academic, you know? Not meant for real life. For real people, I mean. Not meant for you."

Not meant for me...

"You don't have to do this," she whispered. "You can leave. Warn the others. Save the world and leave us here."

He was shaking his head before she finished. "Some people are worth risking the world for," he said simply.

His hand found hers and squeezed it.

Despite the moment, despite the danger and the very real possibility that they would be playing out his disappearance theory anyway, Heather's heart began to soar.

"When you get him," he whispered, "just hide. They want to leave. They won't look too hard."

Jeff had no way of knowing whether or not this was true, but she appreciated the effort. She squeezed his hand back, choked on the lump in her throat, and said, "Don't get caught."

"Of course not," he said, with some of his old humor. "I'm on the track team, remember?" But he betrayed himself with a glance at his ankle. "Whatever happens, don't let them get you."

She couldn't promise him that. If her safety meant leaving either Nick or Jeff behind, she knew she couldn't do it. She couldn't face her parents or Jeff's dad and tell them, *But they made me promise...* She couldn't live with herself. Either all three of them were going home or none of them were.

"Jeff..." she started, but was cut off when the engines roared again. They sounded strong and sure, like lions poised for an easy kill.

They were running out of time.

Jeff stood and hauled her upright too. "Just go get him and get out," he said. "I'll be all right. See you on the other side, Miller."

She nodded. She wanted to say something, anything, but her throat had closed up and her mouth froze. So, instead, she reached up and grabbed his shirt collar. Pulling his face down to her, she threw both arms around his neck and kissed his cheek.

"See you later, Jeffrey Levinson," she whispered in his ear. Then, before she lost her nerve, she turned and ran down the side of the hill, keeping to the bushes so she wouldn't be seen.

CHAPTER 21

The brush and brambles were thick along the ridge and Heather had difficulty keeping from tripping. She raced down the ledge to the level of the clearing, where the brush thinned out, though the thick vegetation remained. Weeds grew here, dry and hard from the chilling fall weather. Thorns scratched through her jeans and stalks as high as her knees in some places curled around her legs like living snares.

Heather pressed on. The line of bushes that Jeff had indicated stretched like a peninsula through the grassy sea, ending about ten yards short of the landing site. This brush would protect her from the sight of the aliens at the landing site, but if any came from the woods stretching behind her, she would be completely exposed. There was no way of avoiding that risk and, anyway, all the aliens were in the ship or behind it.

Heather reached the last cluster of bushes and dropped. Her heart pounded and her hands were trembling and slick with sweat. The pistol was a dead weight in her left hand; she switched it to her right and wiped her palm on her jeans. Whatever happened, she had to keep the pistol in her grip. It was her one protection, with only four bullets and a shaky hold...

She let go of that thought, allowing herself the luxury of a prayer: *Lord, please, may it not come to that…*

The engines cut abruptly, startling her. From the woods somewhere, she heard chittering and the patter of small feet and shifted in her stance. In all the excitement, she'd forgotten about the native-born predators that Nick had seen signs of earlier. Animals would be smarter than to come to the ship, of course, but they would be around on the long trek back to the truck. Another reason not to waste any ammunition.

Her legs began to cramp in her crouching position. The wind came and whipped around her shoulders, lacing her with ice.

Come on, Jeff.

She panicked when she realized they hadn't agreed upon a signal for her to advance. Then she chided herself, thinking, *The signal will be when the aliens move out to investigate the sounds. Now would be a good time, Jeff, now that the engines are…*

All thoughts stopped when a huge bulky shape appeared in the side of the ship. The Hunter was coming out for another armload.

By this point, Heather should have become accustomed to the creatures. She was not. Closer now than she had been for hours, she'd almost forgotten the size and bulk of the creature, the menacing movement of the blackened jaw, the nervous flexing of the hands, the smooth, green-gray skin, the eyes that were like wells, dark and bottomless and lacking any recognizable emotion. They were like lizards, but not. Like panthers, yet not. They were so foreign, so distant, so far from being understandable that the very sight of one was enough to drain every bit of warmth from Heather's body.

They were alien.

They had Nick. And in a moment, they'd be after Jeff.

This is such *a bad idea…*

The Hunter stood in the light for a moment, flexing its arms, scanning the forest beyond, liquid eyes skimming over Heather's hiding spot without pausing. It chittered, the tone cutting like a buzz saw through the relatively still night. Then it listened, cocking its head, and Heather thought, *Is it like sonar? Can they see through sound?*

If so, the trees would still provide cover.

Where is Jeff?

The alien chittered again, black jaw moving awkwardly, then it strode forward to where Nick lay among the barrels. It bent over, and when it rose again, Nick's limp body was thrown over its shoulder.

NO!!

If that thing put Nick in the ship, they would never get him out.

The Hunter turned, heading toward the ship.

Heather had begun to rise, bringing the pistol up to bear on the broad back of the creature, when a sudden noise cut through the air. It was a chirruping sound – an awkward, strangled sound from the black forest on the far side of the landing site. It came, Heather noticed, from where Jeff had disappeared to...

The Sentry?

The Sentry had disappeared before she and Jeff split. She'd assumed, as Jeff had, that he had gone around back of the ship with the Mechanic. But what if he hadn't? What if he was in the woods with Jeff? What if...?

The horrifying thought hardly had time to take root when the Hunter, taking a half step away from the ship, sent an answer chirrup into the woods. Its spine was stiff, free hand resting on its weapon. Whatever the chirrup meant, the Hunter was not at peace.

When the answering chirrup came, it was louder, but not as strong and suddenly Heather knew – it wasn't the Sentry that was calling, it was Jeff. He wasn't throwing things. He was luring them, like a bird's call to a hunter's blind.

The Hunter was poised, ready to move forward or back, its eyes scanning, scanning. The Mechanic came around the nose of the ship, also tense, also questioning. They exchanged murmured conversation. Whatever Jeff was saying, it had aroused their suspicions. And where was the Sentry?

Another call came from the woods and the Hunter took a half step forward, moving as if to dump Nick on the ground. The Mechanic stopped it, still listening. As the Hunter made a tiny adjustment to its grip, Nick flinched.

Nick was alive – but still unconscious.

Again, Jeff, again!

Jeff must have been watching, because this time the chirrup was louder, like a scream in a foreign tongue.

Chirruuuuu! Chirruu, chirruu, chirruu!

It sounded desperate and now there were thrashing sounds, like a body wrestling with a creature. Or, more likely, Jeff using a large branch to make thrashing sounds in the woods.

Whatever he was doing, it worked. The Mechanic started towards the woods, pulling its weapon and snapping an order back at the other alien. The Hunter turned and tossed Nick at the side of the ship. Heather was about to scream, but Nick sailed through the solid wall without a sound. The Hunter pulled its own weapon and darted into the woods. From the speed with which the two aliens moved, Jeff didn't have much time to get out of their way.

Heather didn't allow herself to think about him or anything else. She barely allowed time for the Hunter to get past the first line of trees before she was up on her feet, running to the ship. The pistol weighed heavily in her hand as she ran, her legs pumping, her boots hitting the uneven ground solidly, cutting through the thick weeds. Heather Miller was no track runner, but she crossed that field like a champ.

The ship loomed over her, a reddish-grey anomaly. Heather leapt lightly over some boxes and reached for the side of the ship. She hadn't taken her eyes off the section of the ship into which Nick had been so rudely thrown. She reached out – and made contact with solid metal.

"No. No!"

She didn't know if she was crying out loud or if the screams were just in her head. She ran both hands across the metal, the gun barrel scraping against it, searching for an opening, begging for one. But there was none. It was as solid as it appeared.

"Nick! Nick!"

From the forest beside her, thrashing sounds and grunts indicated a chase, if not a capture. She had moments to get him out, to get free of the clearing before they returned. And Nick was trapped behind a solid wall of metal.

Frustrated, frightened, ready to lose it, Heather bent down, grabbed a rock, and heaved it at the side of the ship. "OPEN UP, DAMN IT!"

The rock pinged off the side of the ship and ricocheted into the darkness.

Heather hardly had time to register that when another sound exploded behind her, only yards away.

Chirree! Chirree! CHIRREE!!

Something was screaming out in pain and fear, something alien. A body appeared at the opposite end of the clearing. The Sentry was running right for Heather, screaming, frightened – but before she could move, another howl ripped through the air. This one was familiar, nightmarish; the Sentry stumbled at the sound. Before he could recover his balance, a body crashed into him, then another, pulling the Sentry to the ground in a tangle of arms, legs, paws, claws, and fur.

The shifting patterns of light and darkness, as the clouds raced across the moon, made it hard to make out what was happening. The Sentry screamed, the coyotes answered. Then the sky cleared. The Sentry was on his belly, splayed out across the ground like a wriggling corpse, his jaw moving as he cried out for help. One coyote had claws in his back; the other was attacking the alien's face. With a vicious swipe of its fore-paw, the coyote ripped open the Sentry's face, sending the black jaw flying. The jaw skittered across the ground until it came to a rest a foot from where Heather stood, agape with fear and fascination.

Heather's stomach lurched.

The alien cry was agonizing and clear. The coyote lowered its head for the kill. The Sentry wriggled, helpless, wheezing piteously. The crack of Heather's pistol cut through all the other chaos.

The first slug hit the first coyote in the shoulder, the weight of the impact jerking it almost off balance. With a yowl that sounded almost human, the coyote raised its dripping jaw to look at Heather. Its claws were still in the back of the Sentry, who had frozen at the unfamiliar sound. The Sentry's labored breathing was the only indication that he was still alive.

The second coyote turned to growl at Heather, ears flat, eyes narrow, growling low and dangerous. Heather fired again.

Where she hit this time, she couldn't have said, but it must have struck home. They both jumped off the alien, heading right for her. Heather shouted, but didn't have time to move before she was rammed into by a warm mass of flesh and muscle. She went down backwards, barely keeping her head enough to tuck and roll back up onto her knees. She raised her head and the pistol just in time to see the coyotes hightailing it for the woods, one limping and crying in pain.

Suddenly they were gone and all that could be heard was the thunderous beating of Heather's heart and the painful, gasping wheezing of the wounded alien.

That was a close call...

There was something rather ironic about the small alien almost being eaten by an Earth-bound predator, but Heather didn't take time to dwell on it or the fact that she'd just expended two bullets trying to save one of the enemies who'd taken Nick. The Sentry was crying, his wheezing growing more and more labored. Heather climbed shakily to her feet and approached the gasping alien, keeping a safe distance away and her finger on the trigger.

The Sentry was curled into a fetal position. His chest rose and fell in ragged movements, his breath labored and growing worse by the second. He looked up at Heather, dark eyes almost invisible in the night's light, and moaned. One hand-claw lifted weakly, waving her off. Blood, thick and black, crawled down the alien's limb.

He's dying.

But the Sentry wasn't just dying from wounds. He was wheezing, like Greg Moran did when his lungs closed up from asthma.

But why...?

Heather's foot brushed up against something hard, something unnatural. She looked down and saw the jaw the coyote had ripped off in its attack. But it wasn't made of flesh - it was made of light metal. When she snatched it up, it weighed a decent amount in her hand.

This wasn't a jaw. It was a breathing mask.

They can't breathe our air, she thought. *This little guy is suffocating.*

Of all the things she, Nick, and Jeff had had to consider that long, exhausting day, this particular weakness had never even occurred to them.

They are partially blind and can't breathe our air...

The Sentry's pleading whine cut through her revelation. Fluttering hands reached weakly for the mask. His rasping breath ripped through Heather's defenses and before she could quite consider all the ramifications of her actions, she tossed the mask to the alien.

He fumbled for the mask like a drowning man reaches for a float, and shoved it into his face. The expression of relief was almost human. Despite everything that had happened tonight, Heather felt a twinge of pity and relief.

Chirruu. Cheeeeerruuu...

The call, ripping through the unnatural quiet, did not originate from the Sentry. Heather snapped to, pulling up the gun and aiming at the wounded alien, who squeaked at the movement but was still too wounded to move.

"One move and I'll kill him," Heather called out. She couldn't possibly be understood, of course, but it felt better to say it out loud. "Stay right where you are..."

Then she saw them. The Hunter and the Mechanic stood on the edge of the clearing. The Hunter was straining forward, eyes focused on Heather and the gun, while the Mechanic stood, restraining its companion.

They'd returned. And the only thing standing between Heather and annihilation were two bullets in a forty-five automatic.

CHAPTER 25

The pistol felt like it weighed fifty pounds. Heather stood, her gaze flicking between the Sentry on the ground and the crewmates in front of her. Stalemate – at least, stalemate for as long as the aliens wanted their crewman back.

Do they have loyalties? Will they care if I kill him?

In apparent answer to her question, the Hunter crouched as though to spring, its powerful muscles rippling, a muffled growl filling the night air. Heather's heart stopped, but the Hunter's forward motion was choked by the Mechanic, who shrieked a warning and yanked its crewman back and around to face it.

Heather breathed. The Sentry, only a yard away, whimpered, drawing Heather's attention. He had curled into a ball, holding the mask with one hand, the other hugging himself like a frightened child. His eyes met Heather's and he whimpered again, louder this time, and the sound reminded her of a wounded sheep.

He's frightened of me, Heather thought. She rode a brief wave of confidence before the next thought knocked her back down again. *What do I do now?*

The Sentry's bleat caught the attention of the other two aliens. Now the Mechanic moved, uttering a cry similar to the Sentry's. This time, though, Heather was ready for them. She stepped forward, jerking the gun to show it, and screamed, "One step and *I'll blow his head off!*"

The aliens might not have understood the words, but they could read body language. The Hunter stopped the Mechanic, wrapping one arm around its companion while looking ready to spring on Heather, talons spread and ready. The Sentry squeaked and curled into an even tighter ball, his wounds weeping.

They stood for a moment, the four of them, caught in an uneasy draw. Heather, the smallest and the weakest, held the high card, but only as long as they feared the gun. She drew a deep breath, trying to think of her next move; in the time it took for her to draw that breath, the Mechanic, holding on to the side of the Hunter as though for dear life, uttered a little cry. The Sentry responded. And suddenly, Heather saw and understood, clearly and for the first time, what exactly she was in the middle of.

In the midst of this world-shaking new knowledge, Jeff's voice came crisply and quietly through the night air.

"Heather!" Heather's head jerked in the direction of his voice. "Heather! *Prisoner exchange!*"

The Hunter and the Mechanic started at that. The Hunter loosened his hold on the Mechanic, turning towards Jeff's voice while the Mechanic remained facing Heather, hands wringing in terrified frustration. The Sentry's peril had distracted them from Jeff, but now they must have wondered if he had a weapon too.

The Hunter looked ready to charge and Heather found herself shrieking again: "Hey! *Hey!*"

The Hunter halted, looking uncertain. The Mechanic looked from him to the Sentry. The stand-off resumed.

Jeff's disembodied voice came again. "Prisoner exchange, Heather!"

She nodded, then cleared her throat. The eyes of all the aliens were on her now.

"Hey!" Heather jabbed the gun at the Sentry, causing the two larger aliens to tense up – then she pointed to the ship. "Give me Nick," she said. "And I'll let him go."

She brought the gun back to bear on the Sentry.

There was stillness for a moment. The Hunter looked from the Sentry to the woods where Jeff's voice came from. The Mechanic looked from the Sentry to the ship, then to Heather. There was something in the Mechanic's face or posture that made Heather think she was asking a question. So Heather did the motion again.

"My brother for your guy here. My brother, your guy. We go home."

The Hunter made a motion as if to spring when the gun was pointed away from the Sentry, but the Mechanic grabbed his arm, stopping him yet again. The Mechanic muttered faint chirrups, rubbing the Hunter's arm while he, still tense and ready to kill, glared balefully at Heather.

Heather's arm was getting sore. Sweat poured down her sides, making her shirt stick to her torso. Her nerves were taut, but her grip on the gun was good and, for once, she felt ready and steady. She jabbed the gun at the Sentry again and, when she had their attention, she pointed to the ship.

"My brother. *Now.*"

This time, the Sentry chirruped, too.

The Hunter's eyes were bottomless dark pools that offered nothing but pain and death. The Mechanic was appealing now, not to Heather, but to him. Heather could tell from the change in tone and body language. If the Mechanic had been human, Heather would have said she was close to a meltdown.

The wind whispered around Heather's shoulders, bathing her in chill. Practically underneath her, the Sentry quivered – whether in fear, in cold, in pain, or in combination of all three, Heather didn't know. She kept the gun steady and her voice loud enough to be heard across the clearing.

"You've got ten seconds to bring out my brother," she announced.

Four sets of eyes watched her. It was impossible to tell how many were comprehending. At the corner of her eye, Heather noticed unnatural movement in the trees just outside the ring of light cast by the aliens' equipment. Jeff was making his way towards her. It was too much to hope that he had a back-up plan.

"Ten seconds," Heather repeated, keeping her voice firm. "Ten."

The aliens stared. No movement. No idea, maybe, of what she was saying, so Heather made the gun jerk with each count.

"Nine. Eight…"

Sweat beaded on her brow. Still the aliens stared, the Sentry whimpering, the Mechanic tightening her hold on the Hunter.

"Seven. Six…"

This isn't working!

She had no other plan. If they didn't act, what could she do? Stand there until dawn streaked the sky? Shoot the Sentry and hope she had time to down another alien before they got her?

But even as she considered it, Heather heard the Sentry's whimper and knew she couldn't kill him. Maybe the others, but not him.

"Five…"

She was screaming the numbers now, fear and powerlessness fueling every word. If they didn't understand the language, they *had* to understand the desperation.

"Four… Three…"

Oh God, oh God, oh God…

The Sentry cried out, a wheedling, painful, pathetic cry. He knew, even if the others didn't understand.

"TWO…"

The Mechanic moved then, shocking everyone with her sharp chirrup and sudden punch to the Hunter's shoulder. The Hunter turned and the Mechanic gestured wildly. Heather's heart stopped and in the brush behind the Sentry, she heard Jeff's breath catch.

The Mechanic was gesturing towards the ship.

For once, the Hunter didn't argue with her. With a grunt strong enough to shake the ground around him, he turned sharply and walked into the side of the ship.

Heather couldn't breathe. She couldn't think. She could barely feel the gun in her hands and only just stopped herself from dropping it. When the Hunter appeared with Nick slung over his shoulders, she had to stop herself from crying out.

It had worked. She'd *communicated*!

"Careful, Heather!"

Jeff's voice brought her up sharp with reality. The Hunter had walked the few steps between the ship and the Mechanic and now he stood alongside his crewmate, waiting.

Now came the tricky bit. Working the exchange.

"Jeff," she said, keeping her gun on the now-silent Sentry. "I'm going to need you."

"Right."

Jeff started to lurch out of the bushes and she hissed, "Easy, easy!"

He stopped, then advanced slowly, until he stood on the edge of the ring of light.

The aliens were uneasy. Their eyes shifted from the humans to the Sentry and back again. The Hunter was clearly unhappy, the Mechanic too concerned with the smaller alien to care. She gestured from Nick to the Sentry and back again. The exchange was still going to happen.

Heather nodded slowly and said to Jeff, "Nick's still unconscious. I'm going to need you to grab him, right?"

"Right." He held out his arms willingly.

"Step further away from me."

"Right."

Jeff did as he was told. Heather took one step back from the Sentry, then another, but kept her gun on his head. With her other hand, she gestured to Nick, then to the ground in front of Jeff, and back again.

"Here," she said. "Put him there."

The aliens were still.

Heather gestured again. "Put him there." Then she pointed from the Sentry to the pair and back again. "Bring Nick here and take your comrade."

Again, it was the Mechanic that made the connection and who gestured to the Hunter. Despite her instructions, the Hunter stood still and glowered at Heather, clearly distrustful. He didn't want to come close. Which made sense, because Heather didn't want to get any closer to him herself.

As an act of good faith, she took another step and this time raised the pitch of her voice, hoping to get some action by sounding crazy. "Do you *hear* me? Bring him *here!*"

She made a jerking motion towards the Sentry, who squealed in terror. Finally the Hunter moved. Step by lumbering step, he moved toward Jeff and his outstretched arms. But his eyes never left Heather's face and the black mask moved as of its own accord.

Finally, the alien's bulky form loomed up over Jeff, but he didn't twitch. He looked up at the alien without blinking, and said, "If you would…"

The alien shrugged and Nick's body slipped to the ground, hitting it hard. The Hunter took a step back and looked to Heather as Jeff moved forward.

Heather took three steps back and gestured with the gun.

In two leaping bounds, the Hunter was by the Sentry, pulling the smaller one up by the arm, checking him over for wounds. The Sentry chittered nervously, one hand holding the mask over his face. Satisfied, the Hunter thrust the little one behind him and turned to face Heather again. The Mechanic called out and the Sentry began to stagger toward the ship. The Mechanic met the Sentry half-way, wrapping him in her arms.

The Hunter was now between Heather and the ship and the crewmen. Heather kept her pistol and her eyes on him.

"Jeff?" she said, shifting her stance. "Can you move him?"

"I can't tell if there's a concussion…"

"Jeff! Can you move him?"

"Heather…"

It wasn't Jeff who spoke her name.

Nick!

In her shock and surprise, Heather took her eyes off the Hunter.

"Heather, don't-" Jeff warned, but his voice was lost in the Hunter's roar.

A blow, heavy and solid like an oak falling, caught Heather around the midsection, knocking her off her feet and the breath from her body. Her feet left the ground and she landed a few feet away on her back, blinking back unconsciousness, the roar in her ears almost as loud as the cacophony of sound in the clearing. The pistol was lost and before she could clear her head enough to look for it, something solid landed on her chest, pinning her to the ground. The blurry night sky overhead disappeared behind the massive black bulk hovering over her. The weight of the Hunter's foot pressed down on her chest, screaming pain forgotten in the sudden panicked need to breathe.

Something chittered by her ear. The Hunter was talking. Heather gasped and squirmed, but it was like trying to get out from under the Empire State Building. She could feel the talons as they gripped her chest through her jacket, felt the shift of weight as the Hunter raised an arm for the killing blow, the warmth of his body competing with the cold that was leaching into hers from the ground.

From a great distance, she heard Jeff shouting, terrified and angry. She could feel the rocks and rough ground pressing into her back. Her head filled with a swarm of angry bees and only dimly through that mass of sound and terror and sure knowledge of coming death could she hear herself pleading, "I can't breathe, can't breathe..."

The talons tightened. The Hunter began to swing. Heather closed her eyes...

And a sound exploded through the air.

"CHIRRRRRUPPP!"

As suddenly as it had come, the weight on her chest disappeared. The talons ripped at her jacket as they were viciously torn away and the angry chirrup was repeated, this time so close to Heather that she thought her ears would burst at the pressure.

She opened her eyes. The Hunter was gone. The Mechanic stood over her now, taloned hands clenching and unclenching with anger and frustration. But she wasn't looking at Heather. She was looking over Heather, to where the Hunter was picking himself off the ground. A few yards away, Jeff stood stock-still in the place he'd run to in a futile effort to save Heather, staring open-mouthed at these new developments. Behind him, Nick struggled to rise.

Heather tried to speak, tried to warn Jeff to run, but her lungs were raw with the effort of dragging oxygen in and she couldn't find her voice.

The Hunter roared in anger. The Mechanic met it with scolding. Their voices rebounded off the trees like thunder. The Hunter made as though to charge Heather again. Before Heather could attempt to roll, the Mechanic was moving, stepping *over* Heather to argue with the Hunter. It was a *defensive* move.

What the…?

Jeff was at her side, then, grabbing her shoulders. "You okay?" he asked.

"I'm… get out… Get Nick out…"

But his grip on her shoulders only tightened.

"Not without you, Heather. I promised."

Even as the words left his lips, the two aliens turned to them. Jeff started to rise, but Heather grabbed his sleeve and pulled him back down.

"No," she said. "Wait."

The Mechanic was still arguing. The Hunter looked… sullen. The Mechanic gestured to the ship, to the Sentry, then to Heather. When that didn't work, she reached up and pulled off her own breathing mask to wave it in the Hunter's face. Her wheezing filled the clearing. Immediately, the Hunter snatched the mask and shoved it into the Mechanic's face, chirruping softly.

There was a moment of absolute silence. The two aliens stared at each other as though communicating without words.

Jeff's hands were strong on her shoulders, his breath regular and even. He was waiting. She was waiting. The whole world waited.

By the ship, the cowering Sentry whimpered softly and broke the spell. The two aliens pulled apart and when they swung around to face Heather, Jeff, and the ship, Heather could feel Jeff tense up again. When the aliens lumbered forward, she closed her eyes.

But the teens didn't die that night. One set of heavy feet lumbered solidly around them, heading sullenly to the ship. The other stopped in front and Heather could feel the hot breath of the alien as she bent in front of them.

Chirrup...

The word was almost gentle.

Heather found herself looking into the eyes of the Mechanic. The alien face was unearthly, foreign, with eyes that appeared to belong to insects rather than any animal. Yet, even so, there was something recognizable in them. Something that pinned Heather down and made her almost strain to see.

Behind them, the Hunter called to the Sentry and the tinny sounds of feet and talons on metal told Heather that someone had boarded the ship. The engines started with a smooth, low rumble. Oddly, she wasn't afraid. Looking up at her one-time attacker, one-time savior, Heather realized something. The Mechanic might be alien, but she was not necessarily a monster.

"Chir-chir-chirrup," the Mechanic rumbled softly. "Chir-rup."

The words meant nothing to any human, but Heather nodded anyway.

"You're welcome," she whispered.

From behind them, the Hunter roared, a warning call. The Mechanic rose and leapt over the human pair in one swift movement. When Jeff and Heather turned, Heather grunting against the pain of the movement, it was just in time to see the Mechanic disappear into the side of the ship.

The ship rose with the ease of a helium-filled balloon. They watched it rise higher and higher until it rested some distance above the trees, a rumbling reddish-log of a ship, shimmering in the moonlight. And then it vanished without warning. The three humans were alone in the middle of the clearing.

Heather collapsed against Jeff, letting him hold her without shame; it was some time before he found the voice to speak.

"What," he asked, "was *that?*"

Heather sighed and tightened her grip on his arms.

"That," she said, "was a family. Father, child, and mother."

There was a pause. Then Jeff said, "Well. I'll be darned."

Somewhere in the darkness, Nick's voice, weak and annoyed, began to grow louder amid the normal night noises.

"...like I was hit by a friggin' bus or something, trying to get that stupid camera..."

This time, Heather didn't cry. This time, she laughed.

EPILOGUE

"**A**lien."

It was a statement, not a question. The forest ranger stood at the end of Heather's bed, arms folded, hat pushed back on his forehead, disbelief writ large across his weathered face. One by one he'd taken each of the hikers aside and questioned them alone, starting with Nick because he knew Nick from his summer job. With each interview, the sour look on his face had grown steadily until now he looked as though he'd just downed the contents of a dill pickle jar on a dare and was minutes away from bringing it all back up again.

"Aliens," Heather corrected. Her throat was sore and she took another sip of the juice her mother had given her. "There were three of them."

"Little green men?"

Heather gave him a dirty look.

"There was *nothing* little about them," she said. "And they weren't exactly green. More like camouflage."

The ranger's eyebrows knitted together. He merely nodded and jotted notes on his pad. The disbelief grew more prominent on his face and Heather thought, *If only we'd found that camera.*

She and Jeff had spent almost an hour in the clearing, searching for that camera by moonlight. They'd combed through every inch of ground while Nick, recovering from some kind of head trauma, fought dizzy-spells and nausea attacks. Thorough though they'd been, the camera was gone. Jeff thought it likely that it had been left behind on the ship.

"Nice souvenir of our planet," he'd said.

"That and the deer," Heather replied, and both shivered at the memory.

"There's one small consolation," Jeff continued. "It was a fresh roll of film. All they have are my magnificent photos of the great outdoors."

"Meaning?"

"Meaning no information about humans, our military capabilities, or weaponry. It's as harmless as a *Ranger Rick* magazine."

Heather smiled broadly. "Well," she said. "I hope they enjoy the picture of the inchworm."

"If they have any art in their soul," he pronounced soberly, "it'll move them deeply."

When Nick's symptoms subsided to a reasonable level, they'd started the hike back. Between Nick's nausea, Jeff's ankle, and Heather's bruised ribs, it was slow going. Yet somehow in that time, they became a team. Nick directed them, while Heather kept an eye on security and on their wounds. But it was really Jeff that got her through the night. Somehow, the boy who'd been afraid to face bears and coyotes was the one who could make an alien invasion seem both normal and manageable. His steady stream of observations, and jokes, his cheerful resilience, and willingness to do whatever needed to be done buoyed her spirits and kept her fear of the dark at bay.

Dawn broke before they found the truck. They'd just gotten in, with Heather in the driver's seat, when the first band of rescuers, including Nick and Heather's dad, and their cousin George Miller, and two rangers found them.

That was the first time they gave the explanation. The second time was when they first reached the cabins, just after Heather's mother, a ghostly wreck of her usual lively self, came running out to meet them with the aunts and grandmothers following close after.

Now Heather was safely ensconced in her room at the cabin, luxuriating in the soft feel of the coverlets and pillows. Her hands were sore, her back was sore, her legs were sore, her chest ached from internal bruising, and, if her Aunt Linda were to be believed, everything would hurt worse tomorrow.

Aunt Linda was there now, having refused to leave while she was in the middle of treatment. A trained emergency room nurse, she'd seen to each of the kids in succession, starting with Nick (at the insistence of both Jeff and Heather) and ending, now with Heather.

Aunt Linda may have been experienced, but she'd gasped when she saw the talon marks on Heather's stomach and chest.

"Heather!" she'd exclaimed. "What on earth made these?"

"Aliens," Heather had tiredly explained. "One of them put his foot on my chest."

To Heather's surprise, Aunt Linda hadn't argued with her. She treated the wound and then called for her husband.

Uncle Bill Emery was a cop, formerly in Boston, now in Manchester. According to Heather's mother, Bill's sister, he was the early proto-type for Nick – gregarious and passionate and full of energy. He stood silent now, leaning against the wall with his arms folded, watching the ranger narrowly as Aunt Linda continued to tend to Heather. His salt-and-pepper hair was rumpled from the long night's search. Heather supposed he was as skeptical as the ranger. Why shouldn't he be? They had no proof, aside from the talon marks, to show them.

Heather must have given a sign of her growing distress, for Aunt Linda took her hand and gave it a reassuring squeeze. Aunt Linda was as calm and cool as Uncle Bill was a force of nature. She showed no signs of either skepticism or acceptance of the story, yet Heather was still glad for her presence. Jeff and Nick were outside, talking with their parents and cousins, no doubt making as little progress there as she was making here.

"I don't suppose," the ranger said, still writing, "that this ship had a license number or anything?"

Uncle Bill snarled, "Harvey..." in a warning tone.

"It did," Heather said firmly. "But we couldn't read the lettering. It was... well, alien."

"Alien lettering. Of course..."

His pencil scratched across the pad. The silence in the room was overwhelming, yet, despite this, despite knowing that no-one would believe them, that this incident would pass without comment, Heather felt a strong sense of peace. Nick knew and he was joining the military. Jeff knew and he was going into the sciences. She knew and she would find some career in a similar field. The three of them knew and they would keep watch. Hopefully, that would be enough. And the aliens, though strange and frightening, were not quite as *alien* as they'd thought. And if the aliens could be reduced to human terms, then the Russians couldn't possibly be as big a threat as everyone thought.

I was right. Mom and I were right.

The sun was warm and comforting, falling in a shaft across Heather's bed. She was slipping off into sleep when the door opened and Heather's dad came in.

"How's she doing?" he asked Linda, his dark eyes alert. He sat on the side of the bed and patted Heather's arm awkwardly. Heather moved to lean against him.

Aunt Linda smiled. "She's fine, James, but I want to get them all checked out at the hospital as soon as we can get them there."

"I have a few more questions," the ranger said and Uncle Bill groaned, "Yeah, we know, Harvey."

The door opened again and Jeff appeared, limping on his home-made crutches. He smiled when he saw Heather, and Heather smiled back. Even covered in bruises and cuts, his hair wild from changing, his ankle swathed in enough gauze to wrap a house, Jeff Levinson was still the cutest boy Heather had ever seen in her entire life.

Heather Levinson, she thought and decided she liked that.

Nick came stumbling in after him, his bruised face crinkled in a frown that looked an awful lot like Uncle Bill's. Mr. Levinson was on his heels, looking worried.

Heather's mother came in next. "What is this, a convention?" she asked.

"I'm just wrapping up here, Mrs. Miller," the ranger said.

Jeff sat at the foot of Heather's bed, leaning his crutches on the mattress. Nick sat next to him and fixed him with a firm, *Not too close* look.

"Well," Nick said, and winced as he turned to look at the ranger. "The gang's all here."

"Yes." Mr. Levinson was anxiously rubbing his hands, his eyes moving from one face to another. Heather felt bad for him. Here he was, surrounded by people he barely knew, all of whom were instrumental in putting his only son in a position where he might have been killed. It was surprising that Mr. Levinson was speaking to them at all.

"What's our next move?" he asked.

The ranger shrugged, closing his notebook. "Get these kids some proper... to a proper hospital," he corrected, avoiding Uncle Bill's savage scowl. "File a report of missing persons found with the department. File it and forget it. No harm, no foul."

"No *harm*," Mr. Levinson said and pointed to his son's ankle. "What do you call that?"

"People get hurt hiking all the time, Mr. Levinson. It's not unusual."

"These circumstances are hardly *usual.*"

The ranger gave him a look. "It's been a long day, Mr. Levinson..."

"You don't believe them," Aunt Linda declared. She was standing by the bed now, packing her kit. Her normally soft brown eyes were sharp with accusation. "You think my niece and nephew are lying."

Now the ranger shifted uncomfortably. "Come on," he protested. "Alien invaders… I mean, really…"

"My son," Mr. Levinson said firmly, "is not a liar."

The look on Jeff's face was priceless.

"AND," Nick added, pointing to the notebook that sat forgotten in Jeff's shirt pocket. "He's got notes."

The ranger ignored him and turned on Mr. Levinson. "Do you really expect me to believe their story? Little green men, in *our* mountains?"

"Why not?" Uncle Bill said. "It's not the first time they've been reported."

"They have no proof. No evidence. Not a thing to substantiate their story." The ranger drew himself up and faced Uncle Bill, thumbs tucked into his heavy belt. "Do you really expect me to go to the FBI without evidence?"

The room was silent once again. Every face was turned to the confrontation, towards the unusually still Uncle Bill and the irate ranger.

Heather thought, *Why should they believe us? I wouldn't believe us.*

Uncle Bill's eyes shifted, looking over the ranger's shoulder towards his wife. Aunt Linda folded her arms and nodded, as though giving Uncle Bill permission. It was a comfortable exchange, like two weathered agents who'd been through the same drill a million times before.

Uncle Bill pulled himself off the wall he'd been leaning on and looked the ranger dead in the eye.

"Of course I don't expect you to go to the FBI without evidence," he scoffed. "They're pills at the best of times. What I *do* expect from you is an effort to *find* the evidence." He looked past the astonished ranger toward Jeff and Nick. "Think you could find your way back to that landing site, son?"

Jeff started, clearly astonished. Then, before Heather's eyes, he grew about three inches, sitting straight and proud to be called upon. He glanced at his dad as he answered, "Of course I can."

Nick snorted and nudged Jeff. "You wouldn't get half a mile without me, Spock," he said. But there was comradery in his tone and Jeff smiled in recognition of it.

"I'm coming, too," Heather said.

"Count me in," her dad said. "How about you, Dave?"

Mr. Levinson was already nodding.

"Looks like I'd better pack some lunches to go," Heather's mom said. "We could be out there a while."

Warmth flooded Heather's system. They were believed. They were supported. Something was going to be done.

Uncle Bill rounded on the ranger. "All right, then, Harvey," he said. "Better put on your big-boy boots. We're heading back into the woods and we are going to find you that evidence."

With that, he turned and strode out of the room before the stuttering, sputtering ranger could think of a thing to say.

BONUS SCENE:

BOOK ONE of THE ENCOUNTER series:

TALE HALF TOLD

1971

When four friends are trapped in a snow-bound haunted house, the battle isn't just for survival – it's for their sanity...

EXCERPT:

There was in the air a sense of impending battle. Johnny knew it like he knew the scent of napalm. The world was conspiring against them, gathering forces, preparing to strike. The wind was the first line, whipping up the light snow from the ground and sending it, stinging, into their faces as they struggled through the drifts towards the car. Johnny took the lead and Michael brought up the rear. It was not snowing yet, but Johnny could taste it in the air and he did not like it. The storm was moving much too fast.

He pulled open the passenger door and helped Linda in while Susan moved around the front of the vehicle towards her door. Michael stumbled next to him, fumbling for the handle.

"You're right," he said to Johnny, raising his voice to be heard above the wind. "Let's get out of here before a tree falls."

There was an audible sigh of relief when the doors were shut. After turning over twice, the engine started. Michael shifted into reverse and pulled backwards as the wind, roaring in defeat, slammed into the side of the car, causing the entire vehicle to shudder.

"Good grief!" Linda said. "What is with the weather today?"

No one answered her. Michael had gone too deep into the drifts behind them and was gently trying to ease the spinning tires back onto pavement. Susan looked ill again. Johnny found himself sitting at attention as though expecting an attack at any minute.

Stop it, he told himself, and then said aloud to Linda, "It's just the wind coming off the river, that's all. Want me to get out and push, Mike?"

Even as he said it, the tires caught traction and they began moving towards the road.

"We're on our way now," Michael said heartily. "Just a little bit of New England weather."

His white knuckle-hold on the constantly shifting steering wheel belied his confident tone. They knew better than to reply. Even the backseat passengers could feel the shift of the slipping tires while they were still on flat ground. All around them, the wind whipped up the sugar-like snow, casting drifts and fresh layers onto their path.

The driveway was only a few hundred yards long, ending in a sharp downslope to the road. Michael slowed as he reached it, until the tires caught ground and held.

"It's slippery," Susan warned.

Michael said, "I know, honey, I know," as he eased the car forward. They reached the lip of the incline and the car tipped.

"Easy does it…" Michael said, just before the tires touched ice.

The car hurtled down the slope, picking up speed and twisting as Michael fought for control. Johnny braced himself and reached out for Linda, who had one hand clasped to her mouth. Susan was climbing up into her seat, bracing her legs against the dashboard, repeatedly crying, "Michael, the tree! Michael, the *tree!*"

The car turned despite Michael's frantic struggle with the wheel and pounding on the brakes. They slipped down the end of the driveway, slid across the road and tipped over the edge into the ditch. Susan's scream was cut off abruptly when they hit the trees with a crescendo of breaking glass and the bone-crunching sound of metal wrapping around wood.

TALE HALF TOLD

1971

Book One in THE ENCOUNTER series

AVAILABLE NOW ON KINDLE AND IN PAPERBACK

ABOUT THE AUTHORS

Margaret Traynor and **Killarney Traynor** are sisters who live in New Hampshire and have way too much time on their hands. **Margaret** is an EA, travel enthusiast, and coffee fanatic who works in an accounting office during the day and hikes the White Mountains on the weekends. **Killarney** is an author, actress, and bookworm and generally too busy watching black and white movies to hike. *The Encounter Series* is founded in their mutual love of "The Twilight Zone", "X-Files", Agatha Christie, and Alfred Hitchcock.

For more information about *The Encounter Series,* visit www.KillarneyTraynor.com

Made in the
USA
Columbia, SC